Once Upon a Time in India

Captain Corcoran

Once Upon a Time in India

The Marvellous Adventures of Captain Corcoran

Alfred Assollant

Translated by
Sam Miller

Original illustrations by
Alphonse de Neuville

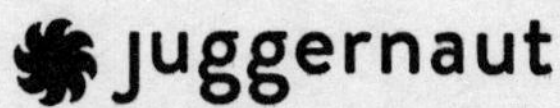

JUGGERNAUT BOOKS
KS House, 118 Shahpur Jat, New Delhi 110049, India

First published as *Aventures Merveilleuses Mais Authentiques du Capitaine Corcoran* Paris 1867
English translation first published by Juggernaut Books 2016

Original illustrations by Alphonse de Neuville

ISBN 9788193237267

For sale in the Indian Subcontinent only

Typeset in Adobe Caslon Pro by R. Ajith Kumar, New Delhi

Printed at Manipal Technologies Ltd

Once Upon a Time in India

Introduction

The other day, a grizzled Parisian bookseller bared his teeth at me, raised his right arm, flexed his fingers and then swiped at my face as if he were a tiger trying to dig his claws into my cheek.

I had been walking along the Seine, visiting the *bouquinistes*, the hundreds of second-hand booksellers who line the right bank of the river, searching for the less well-known works of Alfred Assollant. I was feeling a little disappointed. At stall after stall, they seemed unaware of Assollant's existence. The creator of Captain Corcoran had been forgotten in the land of his birth. And then I met an older bookseller – and I mentioned the name Assollant. And he looked at me in surprise. And he said 'Captain Corcoran' to me. And I nodded, and a huge smile came over his face. 'I haven't heard that name in sixty years,' he told me. 'And I'm seventy-five now.' He loved Corcoran and Sita and Scindia the elephant, but most of all he adored Louison, the ever-hungry tigress – and it was then that he pretended to scratch my face with his tiger claw fingers. He could tell from my accent that I was English – and he remembered that Louison had a particular taste for English blood.

I had come across Corcoran and his pet tiger in 2007. I was living in India then, as was Tony Mango, my wife's stepfather, a ninety-something French-speaking Greek from Constantinople, born under the Ottoman Empire. I had asked him what he knew about India when he was young. Very little, he told me. And what he did know came from what he simply referred to as 'Captain Corcoran', the favourite book of his teenage years. It had created an India in his imagination which was full of tigers, rhinoceroses, elephants, Maharajahs and beautiful, courageous women with lotus eyes. And Tony, like Corcoran, would marry such a woman. When Tony told me about Corcoran, I ordered an ancient copy of the book by post from France – hardbound in red, part of Hachette's *Bibliothèque Rose* series aimed at younger readers. And I lost myself in the adventures of Corcoran, as so many had done before me – including two of the twentieth century's most important political philosophers.

Jean-Paul Sartre recalled in his memoir *Words*, which is principally about the awfulness of his childhood, how the *Adventures of Captain Corcoran* provided him with an escape from that awfulness, almost a redemption. He writes that he read Corcoran perhaps one hundred times – and how the moment he picked up the book, even when he was in middle age, and read its first lines, he could, in his words, 'forget myself' – '*je m'oublie*'.

Antonio Gramsci, too, was an unlikely aficionado of Corcoran. He gave his beloved sister-in-law, Tania, a copy of the Italian translation – *Avventure meravigliose ma autentiche del capitano Corcoran* – in which Louison has been given a more Italian name: Lisotta. Gramsci spent most of his adult life locked up by Mussolini, and in his prison cell he developed his theory of cultural hegemony, and he fantasised about Captain Corcoran. He wrote to Tania imagining her rereading the book he gave her, those 'wondrous stories of Corcoran and his charming Lisotta'.

There is no proper biography of Alfred Assollant (or Assolant as he sometimes signed his name), and we only have sketchy details about large parts of his life. He was born in 1827 in the central French town of Aubusson, better known for its tapestries than its writers. His father was a lawyer; he was the middle child of three – and had a younger sister called Louise, whom I imagine as the inspiration for Louison. Alfred attended the prestigious Ecole Normale Supérieure in Paris, married a woman from Aubusson and became a teacher at a series of provincial schools and colleges.

In 1854 Assollant left teaching. His outspoken republican politics – he was an opponent of France's new ruler, Emperor Napoleon III – made it impossible for him to work as a state employee. Instead, he moved to Paris, took up freelance work as a journalist and writer, and made several unsuccessful forays into politics. He travelled to the United States and to England – and he hated the latter with a passion. He wrote more than thirty books over thirty years: historical fiction, collected essays, a work on the rights of women – but only *Captain Corcoran*, published in 1867, was a success. In the 1870s, his wife, son and daughter died in quick succession – and Assollant found himself poverty-stricken. In 1886 he too died, all but forgotten, in a paupers' hospital next to the Gare du Nord in Paris – despite, and this is a bit of a mystery, the continuing success of *Captain Corcoran*, which was already into its sixth edition.

For at least fifty years after Assollant's death *Captain Corcoran* continued to be widely read – in France and elsewhere – and the book was translated into German, Spanish, Italian, Czech, Polish and Russian – but never English, presumably because of its overt Anglophobia. It was adapted into a successful play for the Parisian stage, and into a radio drama. By the time Sartre and Tony Mango were reading the book in the 1920s, *Captain Corcoran* had been through eighteen editions. And then, probably around the time of the Second World War, it seemed to lose its popularity. *Captain Corcoran* remains in print – but, sadly, is little read these days in France.

~

The *Adventures of Captain Corcoran* is a work of the imagination which, in its humour and excitement, seems to transcend the generations. This is why it endures, in my view, and why it had such a hold on those who read the book in their youth. But it is also very much a tale of its time – of nineteenth-century European colonialism and of Anglo-French rivalry. It was written less than a decade after the events which provide its backdrop: the Uprising of 1857, known to the British as the Indian Mutiny. The British were victorious, and in the aftermath of the Uprising used their position to take direct control of large parts of India formerly under the aegis of the East India Company.

The longer historical context also helps to make sense of

Assollant's book. Until the end of the eighteenth century, France had competed with Britain for control and influence in India. The defeat of Tipu Sultan at Seringapatam in 1799 destroyed all that, and put paid to Napoleon's dream of having an Asian ally against the British. The French 'empire' in India retreated to small coastal or riverine enclaves – and there was undoubtedly some French pleasure in seeing the temporary humiliation of the British in 1857.

Apart from the opening sequence in Lyon, all of *Captain Corcoran* is set in central India – in and around a city called Bhagavpur which resembles the fortified town of Maheshwar on the banks of the Narmada River. Maheshwar was the old capital of the Holkar dynasty (whose name Assollant gives to the princely ruler in *Captain Corcoran*). The Holkars were a real princely family – one of several Maratha (or Mahratta) dynasties. By 1857, they still ruled large tracts of central India from the city of Indore, but had accepted British suzerainty in 1818 following their defeat in the third Anglo-Maratha war. Prince Holkar, in the book, is a dyed-in-the-wool opponent of the British. In reality, the Holkar ruler in 1857, Tukoji Rao II, publicly supported the British, though there were rumours, taken seriously by the British, that he secretly helped the rebels.

Assollant was well read and knowledgeable about Indian history. But he never travelled to India – and there are numerous minor errors in his descriptions of the terrain and vegetation of central India, of Indian customs, of the use of personal names by different groups within and outside the caste system. He recycles existing stereotypes about superstitious Indians who lack courage and physical strength.

However, Assollant's analysis of the dynamics of British colonial activity at the time of the 1857 Uprising – revealed as part of a conversation between Corcoran and the rebel leader Sugriva towards the end of the book – is sophisticated, and he makes it clear that his sympathies lie throughout with ordinary Indians, and not with their rulers.

Assollant makes no attempt to disguise his dislike of the British – or rather the English, as he always refers to them. He visited London in the 1850s, and wrote a long magazine article about it. 'London is ugly, I tell you. It is dirty, it is black. It is made of bricks. It has no real shops, or not ones with displays. It is dark, it is rainy. The prettiest areas are deserted, the others are too crowded.' He continues in this vein for several pages. In *Captain Corcoran* he has his hero declare that 'I care no more for the English than I would for a sour herring or a sardine in oil.' The British, he says, are obsessed with money and protocol – and they get their bloody comeuppance on several occasions in the course of this book.

But Assollant is hardly full of praise for the French, whose scholars are mercilessly mocked in the opening chapter. And later on he attempts to explain to Prince Holkar the difference between the French and the English in terms that are not exactly complimentary about either country:

> There are, in this vast universe, two sorts of men – or, if you want, two principal races – not including yours. They are the French and the English, who are to each other as the dog is to the wolf, or the tiger to the buffalo, or the panther to the rattlesnake. Each of these pairings is hungry – the one for praise, the other for money – but they are equally quarrelsome,

and always ready to meddle in the affairs of the other without being invited.

It is very important to Assollant that the hero of the book is no typical Frenchman. Instead Corcoran is a generous, straight-talking Breton, the son of a fisherman from Saint-Malo – who allows himself to be upstaged at almost every turn by his companion, the wonderful, ever-hungry Louison. They make an unforgettable double act.

Note on the translation: This translation is based on the 1885 Hachette sixth edition of the first volume of *Aventures Merveilleuses Mais Authentiques du Capitaine Corcoran*, the last to be published in Assollant's lifetime (the second volume has not been translated). The text bears several indications of the speed at which Assollant wrote the book, including a number of minor inconsistencies which have been referred to in the notes. The only additions made to the text have been titles for chapters four, five and six, which were omitted for unknown reasons by Assollant. Traditional English orthography had been used for most places and names: so Gouroukaramata becomes Guru Karamta, Sougriva becomes Sugriva, Bhagavapour becomes Bhagavpur, Nerbuddah becomes Narmada, Mahratte becomes Maratha. For publication in the Indian subcontinent the translation has been entitled *Once Upon a Time in India: The Marvellous Adventures of Captain Corcoran*.

Thanks to Jane Miller, Fanny Durville, Urmila Jagannathan and Judith Oriol for their advice and help with the translation.

1

The Academy of Sciences (of Lyon) and Captain Corcoran

It was just before three o'clock on the afternoon of September the 29th 1856, and the Academy of Sciences in the French city of Lyon[1] was in full session. However, every single one of the academicians was fast asleep. It should be said, by way of an excuse, that since midday the celebrated Doctor Maurice Schwartz, of the House of Schwartz, had been reading to them from the shorter version of his Collected Works, telling them about his research on the subject of the footprints left in the dust by the left legs of a hungry spider. And, to be fair, none of the sleepers had given up listening without a fight.

One of them, after having put his elbows on the table, and his head upon his elbows, had begun to sketch a Roman Senator, but drowsiness overcame him at the moment when he started to draw the folds of the toga. Another had constructed an ocean liner from a piece of white paper, and his gentle snoring was like a light wind blowing the sails of his ship. Only the Presiding Officer, leaning against the back of his armchair, slept with any dignity, and he – with his hand on a bell, like a soldier at arms – cut an imposing figure.

But the flow of words continued regardless, as Doctor Schwartz, of the House of Schwartz, lost himself in his infinite considerations on the origins and probable consequences of his discoveries. Then, suddenly, the clock struck three times and everyone woke up. The Presiding Officer began to speak.

'Messieurs,' he said, 'the fifteen chapters of the fine book that we have just heard contain so many new and fruitful truths that the Academy, in paying homage to the genius of Doctor Schwartz, will not be angered, I believe, if I postpone the reading of the following fifteen chapters until next week.'

Once Doctor Schwartz had given his consent to this, it was rapidly agreed that the rest of the lecture should be postponed, and they all began to talk about other things.

Then a small man stood up. He had a beard, white hair, darting eyes, a pointed chin, and he was so thin and gaunt that it was as if his skin had been glued to his bones. He made a sign that he wanted to speak, and everyone was silent, because they knew he was someone who should be listened to and who should not be interrupted.

'Messieurs,' he said, 'our most-honoured and greatly missed colleague, Monsieur Delaroche, died at Suez last month. He was just about to leave for India, to search, amid the mountains known as the Ghats, near the source of the Godavari River, for the *Guru Karamta*, the most important sacred book of the Hindus, long hidden from European eyes.[2] This most generous man, whose memory will always remain precious to those who are friends of science, foresaw his own death, and did not want to leave his life's work incomplete.

He has left one hundred thousand francs to whoever takes on the task of finding this book, of whose existence, according to the Brahmins, there is no doubt.

'Under the terms of his will, this illustrious Academy is responsible for overseeing the legacy, and is therefore responsible for selecting the beneficiary. This choice will be a difficult one, because the traveller whom you send to India must be robust enough to survive the climate, and courageous enough to survive the teeth of a tiger, the trunk of an elephant and the snares of Indian brigands. He must also be cunning enough to deceive the jealous English, whose Royal Asiatic Society[3] of Calcutta has failed so far in its searches, and would not like a Frenchman to have the honour of finding the sacred book. Additionally, the person you choose must know Sanskrit and Farsi, and all the sacred and common languages of India. This is no small matter, and I suggest that the Academy opens up the post to competition.'

This was agreed, and they all proceeded to dine.

Several candidates made themselves known, and canvassed for the votes of the academicians. But the first had too weak a constitution, the second was too stupid, and the third one's knowledge of Oriental languages was limited to Chinese, Turcoman and the purest Japanese. And so several months passed by without the Academy choosing a candidate.

Eventually, on the 26th of May 1857, when the Academy was again in session, the Presiding Officer was handed the business card of a stranger who asked to be admitted.

On the card was the name: Captain Corcoran.[4]

'Corcoran!' said the Presiding Officer. 'Does anyone know that name?'

No one knew the name. But the assembly, which was curious, like all such assemblies, wanted to see the stranger.

The door opened and Captain Corcoran appeared.

He was a large man, barely twenty-five years old, of simple demeanour – with neither modesty nor pride. His face was pale and unbearded. His sea-green eyes seemed to glow with openness and audacity. He was dressed in an overcoat made of alpaca wool, a red shirt and white cotton trousers. The two ends of his necktie, knotted *à la colin*, hung freely on his chest.

'Messieurs,' he said, 'I have learnt that you are in an embarrassing situation, and I have come to offer my services.'

'In an embarrassing situation?' interrupted the Presiding Officer with a haughty air. 'You are mistaken, Monsieur. The Academy of Sciences of Lyon is never in an embarrassing situation, no more at least than any other academy. I would like to know what could possibly embarrass a knowledgeable society which counts among its members, dare I say – quite apart from the man who has the honour of presiding – so many great geniuses, beautiful souls and noble hearts.'

At this point the speaker was interrupted by three salvos of applause.

'If that is so,' replied Corcoran, 'and you have no need of anyone, I will say goodbye.'

He turned round and walked towards the door.

'One second, Monsieur,' the Presiding Officer said to him, 'you seem pretty confident. At least, tell us the subject of your visit.'

'Well,' replied Corcoran, 'you're searching for the *Guru Karamta*, aren't you?'

The Presiding Officer smiled in a manner that was ironic and benevolent at the same time.

'And so you, Monsieur,' he said, 'are going to find the *Guru Karamta*, are you?'

'Yes, I am.'

'You know the conditions of the legacy of Monsieur Delaroche, our wise and much-lamented brother?'

'I know them.'

'Do you speak English?'

'Like an Oxford professor.'

'And can you prove it? Right now.'

'Yes, Sir,' said Corcoran in English, *'you are a stupid fellow.'* He then reverted to French. 'Do you want some other examples?'

'No, no,' said the Presiding Officer, hurriedly. He had never in his life heard the language of Shakespeare being spoken except at the Palais-Royal Theatre. 'It's very impressive, Monsieur. And you also know Sanskrit, I suppose?'

'If one of you would be good enough to ask for a volume of the *Bhagavata Purana*,[5] I would consider it an honour to explain any passage that you should choose.'

'Oh, really,' said the Presiding Officer. 'And Farsi, and Hindustani?'

Corcoran shrugged his shoulders.

'Child's play,' he said.

And immediately, without hesitation, he began to give a speech in an unknown language which lasted for ten minutes. The entire assembly looked at him in astonishment.

'Do you know,' he said, 'what I had the honour of saying to you?'

'I swear by Monsieur Le Verrier's newly discovered planet,'[6] replied the Presiding Officer, 'I didn't understand a single word.'

'Ah, well. It was Hindustani. That's what they speak in Cashmere, Nepal, the kingdom of Lahore, Multan, Oude, Bengal, the Deccan, the Carnatic, the Malabar, Gondwana, Travancore, Coimbatore, Mysore, the land of the Sikhs, Scinde, Jaipur, Udaipur, Jaisalmer, Bikaner, Baroda, Banswara, Nawanagar, Holkar, Bhopal, Baitpur, Dholpur, Satara and the entire length of the Coromandel.'[7]

'Excellent, Monsieur, excellent,' exclaimed the Presiding Officer. 'There is only one other question we have for you. Please excuse my indiscretion, but we are charged, according to the last testament of our dear friend, with a heavy responsibility, which we don't know…'

'Good, good,' said Corcoran. 'Speak freely – but hurry up, because Louison is waiting for me.'

'Louison,' repeated the Presiding Officer with dignity. 'Just who is this young person?'

'She's a friend who comes on all my voyages.'

With these words, the sound of scurrying feet could be heard from the neighbouring room.

Then there was a great noise as a door was slammed shut.

'What's that?' asked the Presiding Officer.

'Louison is getting impatient.'

'Well, she must wait,' continued the Presiding Officer. 'Our Academy is not, I think, at the command of Madame or Mademoiselle Louison.'

'As you please,' said Corcoran.

And seeing an empty armchair which no one had had the

politeness to offer him, he sat down, comfortably positioning himself to listen to an academician who had got up to speak.

Now, the learned academician could not even come up with a few opening words, because someone had forgotten to put water and sugar on the table, and everyone knows that sugar and water are the two sources of eloquence. To correct this unpardonable error, he tugged hard at the bell-pull.

No one appeared.

'The room boy is really very negligent,' the academician said, finally. 'I am going to send for him.'

And he rang the bell twice, thrice, four times, but nobody responded.

'Monsieur,' said Corcoran, taking pity on the tormented bell ringer, 'please do stop. The boy must have quarrelled with Louison and run away.'

'Quarrelled with Louison?' exclaimed the Presiding Officer. 'Is this young person of such bad character?'

'No. Not so bad. But one must know how to deal with her. He must have tried to hurry her. She is so young, and probably became a bit over-excited.'

'So young! What is the age of Mademoiselle Louison?'

'She's five at the most,' said Corcoran.

'Oh, at that age, it's easy to bring them under control.'

'I'm not so sure. She scratches sometimes, she bites…'

'But, Monsieur,' said the Presiding Officer, 'then she should just be put in another room.'

'It's not so easy, you see,' replied Corcoran. 'Louison is independent; she's not used to being thwarted. She was born in the tropics, you see, and I think the heat there may have excited the natural ardour of her temperament.'

'Anyway,' said the Presiding Officer, 'that's quite enough talk of Mademoiselle Louison. The Academy has more important things to do. I return to our questions. Are you of robust health, Monsieur?'

'I suppose so,' replied Corcoran. 'I've had cholera twice, yellow fever once, and here I am. I have my thirty-two teeth, and as for my hair, touch it yourself, and you'll see it's as impressive as a wig.'

'That's good. And you are strong, I hope?'

'Well,' said Corcoran, 'a little less strong than my late father, but enough for my daily needs.'

He looked around him, and seeing the great bars of iron that had been fixed across the window, he took one of them in his hands and, without apparent effort, he bent it – as if it were a stick of red wax softened by the fire.

'What the devil! There's a strapping lad,' shouted one of the academicians.

'Oh, that's nothing,' responded Corcoran quietly. 'If you can show me a 36-pound cannon, I'll happily carry it up that little mountain you have in the centre of Lyon.'

The admiration of those watching was turning to horror.

'And,' continued the Presiding Officer, 'you have experience of the battlefield, I presume?'

'A dozen times,' said Corcoran. 'No more than that. In the seas of China and Borneo, you know, the captain of a merchant ship always has several cannons on board as a protection against pirates.'

'You have killed pirates?'

'Only in self-defence,' replied the mariner, 'and only two or three hundred at the most. I didn't do it alone, and of that number, I personally killed barely twenty-five or thirty of them. My sailors did the rest.'

As he spoke there was another interruption. From the neighbouring room came the sound of one and then several chairs being knocked over.

'This is unacceptable,' exclaimed the Presiding Officer. 'I must find out what is happening.'

'As I said, one shouldn't really irritate Louison,' said Corcoran. 'Do you want me to bring her in here to calm her down? She can't manage long without me, you know.'

'Monsieur,' one of the academicians responded, tartly, 'when one has a child with a runny nose, one must give it a wipe; while an ill-tempered child should be corrected; and one who cries should be sent to bed. But one should never bring such a child into the antechamber of a learned society.'

'You have no more questions?' asked Corcoran without showing any emotion.

'Pardon me, but once more, Monsieur,' said the Presiding Officer as he pressed his gold glasses down on his nose with the index finger of his right hand. 'Are you…? Let us see, you are brave, strong and healthy, that's obvious. You are knowledgeable, and you have proved it by speaking to us in fluent Hindustani, which none of us can understand. But, let's see, are you… how should I put it… sly and cunning? Because you'll have to be to travel in that country of cruel and perfidious people. And, however strong the Academy's desire to award the prize donated by our illustrious friend Delaroche, and however passionate we are about finding the famous *Guru Karamta*, which the English have searched for in vain throughout the entire Indian peninsula, we must consider it a matter of conscience whether we should risk a life as precious as yours, and…'

'Whether I am cunning or not,' interrupted Corcoran, 'I don't know. But I do know that my brain is that of a Breton from Saint-Malo, and the fists that hang from the ends of my arms are unusually strong, and my revolver is of the highest quality, and the steel of my Scottish dirk is without equal. I have not yet met a living being who, once they have laid a hand on me, has escaped unpunished. Cowards are cunning. In the Corcoran family, we just march straight ahead, blasting away like a cannon.'

'But,' said the Presiding Officer, 'what is that terrible noise? I suppose it's Mademoiselle Louison again, amusing herself. Please go and calm her down, Monsieur, and if you can't do that then threaten her with a good beating.'

'Here, Louison, here,' shouted Corcoran without moving from his armchair.

And the door sprang open as if it had been launched from a catapult, and a royal Bengal tiger, of quite extraordinary grandeur and beauty, made her appearance. With one great bound, the tiger leapt over the head of the academicians and landed at the feet of Captain Corcoran.

'Well, well, Louison, my dear,' said the Captain, 'you made a bit of a noise in the antechamber; you disturbed the learned society. That's really not good. Lie down! If you carry on like this, I will no longer take you out in the world.'

This threat appeared to terrify Louison.

2

How the Academy of Sciences (of Lyon) made the acquaintance of Louison

However terrified Louison felt at Captain Corcoran's threat that she would no longer be taken out in the world, she wasn't half as terrified as the members of the illustrious Academy of Sciences (of Lyon). But to be fair to them, it was their profession to be learned people and not to play around with Bengal tigers, and so perhaps one should not resent too passionately their display of human weakness.

The immediate response of the academicians was that they should run to the door, and then into the neighbouring room, from where they might hope to enter the antechamber at the far end of which was a handsome staircase that led out to the street.

From there, they calculated, it shouldn't be too hard to get away – a good foot soldier, after all, if he's not carrying food or luggage, can manage twelve kilometres an hour. Now the house of the academician who lived furthest was little more than a kilometre or two away. So there was a good chance of escaping the company of Louison in just a few minutes.

But however long it might take to write down this scientific reasoning on a piece of paper, the actual decision to flee was taken so rapidly and with such unanimity that in the blink of an eye every one of the academicians had got up and taken flight.

The Presiding Officer himself, even though he was supposed to set a good example, was the nineteenth of the academicians to reach the door which had been seriously damaged by the arrival of Louison.

But no one could cross the threshold. Louison, who did not like being boxed in, saw what they were doing, and decided that she too needed to take some air. And so, in the blink of an eye, and with another great bound, she leapt for the second time over their heads and landed just in front of the Secretary-for-Life, who was hoping to be the first to leave. This venerable man took one step back, and would have taken several more, if the feet of those who were immediately behind him hadn't presented an insurmountable obstacle.

In truth, when they saw Louison in front of them, they all hurriedly retreated, and the Secretary-for-Life ran away, and his wig got a little crumpled in the process.

Louison, meanwhile, was full of excitement, trotting around, and wandering about the room like a young greyhound about to go hunting. She examined the academicians rather closely, her eyes full of mischief, and seemed to be waiting for Captain Corcoran's orders.

The academicians couldn't make up their minds. To leave might not be wise – it would depend on how Louison reacted.

The Secretary-for-Life had let his wig slip onto his shoulder

But to stay might be still worse. So they gathered together and crowded into one corner of the room, piling up the armchairs to make a barricade.

Finally, the Presiding Officer, who was a wise man, at least in so far as we can judge from his words, said out loud that Captain Corcoran should do the honourable thing, and please all of the members of the honourable assembly who were present, and 'buzz off', as he put it, 'by the quickest and shortest route'.

Even though 'buzz off' was not a very parliamentary expression, Corcoran did not take offence, knowing well that there were moments when one did not have the time to choose one's words carefully.

'Messieurs,' Corcoran said, 'I regret most deeply that…'

'Don't just regret. In the name of God, leave,' shouted the Secretary-for-Life. 'I've no idea what Louison thinks of us, but she chills me to the bone.'

Actually, Louison was rather intrigued. In the confusion, the Secretary-for-Life had, without realizing it, let his wig slip onto his right shoulder, in a way that made his head look totally naked to the eyes of Louison, and this new spectacle astonished her.

Corcoran saw all this, and, without saying a word, showed Louison the way by walking towards the exit.

But the door had now been thoroughly barricaded from the outside. And, to make matters worse, it was as if the barricade had been made of bronze, and not even Corcoran could break it down. However, he made such an effort, ramming the door with his shoulder, that the wall shook and the whole building appeared to tremble. He was about to the ram the door a second time when the Presiding Officer asked him to stop.

'It would be even worse,' he said, 'if you brought the building down on our heads.'

'What else can be done?' said the Captain. 'Ah, I can see a way. We can leave by the window, Louison and I.'

The Presiding Officer welcomed this idea very warmly.

'But Captain,' he said, 'take care. First of all, you will need to remove the iron bars. And then it's at least thirty feet from the window to the pavement. Be careful you don't break your neck. And as for your nasty animal...'

'Shush...' replied Corcoran. 'Don't say anything bad about Louison. She is very sensitive. She'll get angry... And as for the iron bars, that's easy.'

And he removed three of the bars without any apparent effort.

'Now,' he continued, 'we can leave.'

In fact, the Academy was divided: between those who feared that Captain Corcoran would break his neck and those who would be only too pleased to see the departure of Louison.

Corcoran sat on the windowsill and got ready to climb down into the street with the help of the sculptures and other protrusions on the outer wall of the building. But then, suddenly, the Presiding Officer called him back.

'Captain,' he said, 'you can't leave us alone with Louison.'

'I wouldn't think of it,' replied Corcoran, 'but I have to go first, because Louison will never jump unless I do.'

'Yes,' continued the Presiding Officer, 'but what if, when you climb down, Louison refuses to jump?'

'The sky would fall before that happens,' responded Corcoran.

'Just make sure Louison leaves first,' said the Presiding Officer.

'Now, that might make sense,' continued Corcoran, 'except that if I picked her up by the neck, and threw her out of the window, Louison, who can be a little capricious, wouldn't wait for me and would start running through the streets. She might perhaps devour ten or twelve people before I could come to the rescue. You have no idea what a big appetite she has. And now it is four o'clock, and she hasn't had her lunch. And normally she has her lunch at one-thirty, just like Queen Victoria… Holy Mackerel! She hasn't had her lunch today. Damn these cursed distractions.'

On hearing the word lunch, Louison's eyes sparkled with pleasure.

She looked at one of the academicians, a fine fellow: healthy, large, plump, fresh and rosy. She opened her jaws wide, and closed them two or three times – and smacked her lips with her tongue in a show of satisfaction. After staring at the academician, she turned towards Corcoran. She seemed to be asking him if it was lunch-time. The academician looked at the two of them and became very pale.

'Well then,' said Corcoran, 'I won't leave… and you, my lovely,' he added while stroking Louison, 'stay calm. If you don't have lunch today, you will have lunch tomorrow, by Jove.'

On hearing this, Louison growled.

'Silence, Mademoiselle,' said Corcoran lifting his whip. 'Silence or I will have to use this on you.'

Was it the Captain's words or the sight of the whip that calmed the tigress? She lay flat on her belly, rubbing her head against the leg of her friend and started to purr like a pussycat.

'Messieurs,' said the Presiding Officer, 'could you all please sit down? If the doors are closed and barricaded it is surely because the doorman has gone to seek help. Be patient and wait, and if you wish, so that we don't waste our time, we can discuss the work of that most knowledgeable of our colleagues, Monsieur Crochet, on the origins and structure of the Manchu language.'

'You talk about Manchu,' grumbled one of the academicians. 'I'll give you Manchu, and all of its compounds and derivatives, and throw in Japanese and Tibetan, if only I could be warming my feet in my own home right now. And have you ever come across a rascal like that doorman? A scoundrel. I will break my walking stick across his shoulders.'

'I think,' suggested the Secretary-for-Life, 'that the honourable assembly is unable just now to exercise the kind of judicious calm which is appropriate for scientific investigations, and it may be appropriate to postpone the discussion of Manchu to another day. Instead, perhaps the Captain would be so good as to tell us about the adventures that first brought him face-to-face with Louison.'

'Yes,' said the Presiding Officer, 'Captain, do tell us about your adventures and especially the story of your young friend.'

Corcoran nodded his head respectfully, and began to speak…

3

A tiger, a crocodile and Captain Corcoran

'Perhaps you have heard, Messieurs, of the celebrated Robert Surcouf, of Saint-Malo. His father was the nephew of the brother-in-law of my great-grandfather. The most illustrious and knowledgeable Yves Quaterquem, member of the Institute of Paris, who discovered, as everyone knows, the method of steering hot-air balloons, is my second cousin. My great-uncle, Alain Corcoran, known as Redbeard, was at college at the same time as the Viscount François de Chateaubriand, and had the honour, on the 23rd of June 1782, between half-past four and five o'clock in the afternoon during the recreation period, of punching the Viscount in the eye. You see, Messieurs, I come from a good family, and the Corcorans can hold their heads high, and look straight into the sun.[8]

'About myself I have little to say. I was born with a fishing line in my hand. I sailed on my own in my father's boat at an age when most children have barely learned the alphabet. When my father died while assisting a fishing boat in distress, I set sail on *The Chaste Suzanne*, of Saint-Malo, which went whaling in the Bering Straits. After three years of travelling towards the North Pole and the South Pole, I changed ships – from *The Chaste Suzanne* to *The Belle Emilie*, and then from *The Belle Emilie* to *The Proud Artaban*, and then *The Son of the Tempest*, a brig which could travel as fast as 18 knots…'

'Monsieur,' interrupted the Secretary-for-Life of the Academy of Sciences (of Lyon), 'you promised us the history of Louison.'

'Please be patient,' replied Corcoran, 'I'm coming to that…'

But the distant sound of drums interrupted him.

'What's that?' asked the Presiding Officer, anxiously.

'I imagine,' replied Corcoran, 'that the frightened porter who barricaded the door went off to get help. What a fool!'

'By Jove,' said an academician, 'it would have been better if he'd left the door open. I don't want to waste my time listening to the history of Louison.'

'Pay attention,' said the Captain, 'this could become serious. They've sounded the alarm bells.'

The bells were ringing in the nearest clock tower, and news of what was happening would now spread as quickly as fire in the wind.

'Great guns!' said the Captain, laughing. 'Things are getting a little hot around here, my poor Louison, especially now that we appear to be under siege in a place that is so well fortified.

'To return to my history, Messieurs, it was towards the end of the year 1853, the same year I had *The Son of the Tempest* constructed in Saint-Nazaire. I was about to unload seven or eight hundred barrels of Bordeaux wine at the port of Batavia in Java.[9] It was good business. So there I was, quite content, for me and my family and my business. But one doesn't have much fun at sea, so I decided that I would go on a tiger hunt.

'You must remember, Messieurs, that the tiger is, in fact, the most beautiful animal in all creation – just look at Louison – but is also, unfortunately, the recipient from God, of an extraordinary appetite. Tigers love to eat beef, hippopotamus, partridge, hare, but what they prefer above all are monkeys, because of their resemblance to humans, and, of course, human beings themselves, because of their superiority to monkeys. And, moreover, tigers can be rather particular, and will never eat the same body-part twice – so, for example, if Louison had devoured the shoulder of the Secretary-for-Life at lunch, nothing would make her eat the other shoulder for dinner. She's as fussy as a bishop's cat.'

The Secretary-for-Life grimaced.

'Honest to God, Monsieur,' continued Corcoran, 'I know that Louison is being foolish, and that the two shoulders are the same, but that's her character, and that can't be changed.

'So I left Batavia, my gun over my shoulder, and wearing big boots like a Parisian out hunting hares on the plains of Saint-Denis.[10] The owner of my ship, Monsieur Cornelius van Crittenden, wanted me to take two Malays along, who would track the tiger. And if the tiger outwitted us, it would be them and not me whom it would eat. But, as you've heard, I am René Corcoran, whose great-grandfather was the uncle of the father of Robert Surcouf, and I just laughed on hearing this suggestion. One is either from Saint-Malo, or not, isn't that right? Now, I am from Saint-Malo, and in all human memory, there has never been anyone from Saint-Malo who has been eaten by a tiger. Incidentally, the opposite is true. It's not often that tiger meat has been served at a Saint-Malo dinner table.

'However, since, after all, I needed help to carry my tent and my provisions, the two Malays followed me, driving a carriage.

'First, several leagues from Batavia, I came across a deep river that went through a monkey forest, as large and as full of carnivorous animals as Paris and its suburbs. And it's in the thickest forest that one finds the lion, the tiger, the boa constrictor, the panther, the crocodile – the most ferocious beasts of all creation – except for man, of course, who kills without need, and for the pleasure of killing.

'By ten o'clock in the morning, it was so hot that even the Malays, accustomed to their own climate, asked to be excused and lay down in the shade. And I stretched out in the carriage, my hand on my rifle in case of a surprise attack, and fell fast asleep.

'A strange spectacle greeted me when I woke up.

'Now, the river on whose banks I had made my camp was called Mackintosh, after a young Scotsman who had made his fortune in Batavia. One day, when he was getting into a boat with some friends, a gust of wind blew his hat into the river. Mackintosh put out a hand to retrieve the hat, but the moment he touched it, a terrifying mouth, which seemed to be part of a large log floating on the river, seized him and dragged him underwater.

'The mouth belonged to a crocodile which had not had its dinner. Futile attempts were made to fish Mackintosh out of the river, and avenge him, but in the end it was left to Providence to punish the murderer.

'The Scotsman's telescope had been hanging from a

shoulder strap across his chest. The crocodile may have been too greedy or too hungry to notice what he was swallowing and so the telescope became lodged, crossways, in the throat of the amphibian, in such a manner that it could not entirely swallow the unfortunate young man, nor resurface from the bottom of the river to breathe. And so it became a victim of its own gluttony. It was found several days later, drowned, by the side of the river, and it had still not let go of the body of Mackintosh.'

'Monsieur,' interrupted the Presiding Officer of the Academy, 'it seems that you have departed significantly from your subject. You promised to tell us the story of Louison, and not the story of the telescope of Monsieur Mackintosh.'

'Monsieur President,' replied Corcoran with deference, 'I'm just coming to Louison.

'It was a little before two o'clock in the afternoon when I was suddenly woken by terrible screams. I sat up, loaded my rifle, and patiently waited for the enemy. The screams came from the two Malays, who were running, terrified, and sought sanctuary in the carriage.

'"Master, Master!" said one of them, "His Lordship is coming, take care."

'"What Lordship?"

'"His Lordship the tiger."

'"That's good. He's spared me the trouble of finding him. Let's see just how terrible his 'Lordship' is."

'As I spoke, I jumped to the ground, and headed towards my first encounter with this new enemy. I still couldn't see the tiger, but could work out where he was from the fear shown by all the other animals, who were fleeing as fast as they could.

The monkeys hurriedly climbed up trees, and from the safety of the treetops they made defiant, mocking faces. Some of them, a little bolder, threw coconuts at the tiger. I could only make out the direction from which he was coming by the sound of the leaves as he brushed and trampled them underfoot. Little by little, these sounds came closer, and since the road was hardly wide enough for two carriages to pass, I began to fear that I would see him too late, and wouldn't have time to react, because the thickness of the forest would completely hide him.

'I realised then that the tiger simply wanted to drink from the river. So that, with luck, he would probably not notice me as he passed by. Eventually, I saw him, but only his profile. His mouth was covered in blood; he looked satisfied, walking with his legs apart like a rich Parisian landlord smoking a cigar on the Boulevard des Italiens[11] after a good dinner.

'He was just ten paces from me. The sound of me cocking my rifle seemed to cause him some alarm. He half-turned his head, saw me on the other side of the bush that separated us, and stopped to think.

'I was following him with my eyes, and in order to kill him from there with one shot it would be necessary to aim at either his forehead or his heart. He stood there, in a three-quarter pose, like a tiger of great importance posing for a portrait photograph.

'In any event, Divine Providence spared me that day from committing a most deplorable murder. Because this tiger, or rather this tigress, was none other than my beautiful and charming friend, the gentle Louison who you see before you now, and who is listening to us with such an attentive ear.

'Louison (for I can now give her that name) had already

dined that day, as I said, and that was a matter of good fortune for me and for her. She thought only of digesting her food in peace. And so, after having looked at me obliquely for several seconds… yes, in the same way she is now looking at the Secretary-for-Life…'

(At which point, the Secretary-for-Life decided to move, and sat down behind the Presiding Officer.)

'Louison continued slowly on her way, and headed towards the river, which flowed past just a few feet away from her.

'All of a sudden, I witnessed a strange sight. Louison who had until then been walking along with an air of magnificent indifference, slowed down. She stretched out her beautiful body, moving forwards close to the ground and taking the utmost precaution to be neither seen nor heard, until she was next to a long tree trunk which was lying in the sand beside the Mackintosh River. I was walking behind her, my rifle at my shoulder, ready to fire, waiting for the right moment.

'But what happened next astonished me. As I got closer to the tree trunk, I saw that it had feet and scales which glistened in the sun, it had eyes that were closed, and a mouth that was open. It was a crocodile lying in the sand under the sun and sleeping like a baby, untroubled by dreams. It snored peacefully, in the way that only a crocodile without a bad conscience will snore.

'And it was probably something about this slumbering crocodile, full of grace and abandon, that inspired Louison to mischief. Her lips opened and she laughed as if she were some young rascal about to play a clever trick on a schoolmaster.

'She carefully edged forward with one of her paws, which she put inside the mouth of the crocodile. She was trying to grab hold of the crocodile's tongue which she thought would make a good dessert. She is fond of desserts; it is a failing of both her gender and her age.

'But she would be severely punished for this bad idea.

'No sooner had she touched the tongue of the crocodile than its mouth closed shut. And its eyes opened – great sea-green eyes, which I can still see in my mind – and which looked at Louison with an air of surprise, of anger and of pain, which it is impossible for me to describe.

'And Louison wasn't very happy either. The poor thing fought like a devil to escape the sharp teeth of the crocodile. Fortunately, she had a good hold on its tongue with her claws, so that the unfortunate crocodile did not dare use all its force to bite off her paw, as it would have done if its tongue had been free.

'It was a battle of equals until then, and I wasn't sure which of them to support. Because, it should be said, after all, that Louison's intentions had not been exactly benign, and her "prank" must have been very disagreeable for her adversary. But Louison – well, she was just so beautiful, so graceful. Her limbs were supple, there was so much variety in her movement. And she was like a kitten, hardly weaned, who should really have been playing in the sun under the watchful eyes of her mother.

'But, alas, she wasn't playing as she twisted around on the sand, her husky cries resounding through the forest. The monkeys, perched in safety high up in the coconut trees, were laughing as they watched this terrifying battle. The baboons pointed out Louison to the macaques, and put their thumbs to their noses and flapped their hands, with the mocking gestures of a Paris street urchin. One of them, more daring than the others, came down, branch by branch, until it was six or seven feet from the ground, and there, hanging by its tail, it dared to scratch, lightly, the head of the redoubtable tigress. Seeing this trick, all the other baboons started to laugh loudly, but Louison responded so quickly and menacingly that the daring young baboon did not dare continue, and considered itself lucky to have escaped the murderous teeth of the enemy.

'Meanwhile, the crocodile was dragging the poor tigress into the river. Louison lifted her eyes upwards, as if to ask for pity or to seek a witness to her martyrdom. And then her eyes fell on me.

'What beautiful eyes! What a sad, soft look which seemed to depict all the anxieties of an impending death! Poor Louison!

'At that moment, the crocodile plunged into the river, dragging Louison underwater. That's when I made my decision. But all I could see now of Louison was the splashing and bubbling of water as she tried to get away. I waited for thirty seconds, my rifle at the ready, my finger on the trigger, my eyes fixed on the river.

'Fortunately, Louison who is an animal, but not, if you know what I mean, a beast, was able, in the midst of her despair, to grab on to the trunk of a tree that hung over the edge of the water. This saved her life.

'She managed, as she struggled, to lift her head above water, and by doing so saved herself from the most immediate danger – that of drowning. After a while, the crocodile also needed to breathe a little, and with a mixture of willpower and brute force dragged them both towards the riverbank.

'This was what I was waiting for. In the blink of an eye it was all settled. I got into position, fired my rifle, sending a

Meanwhile the crocodile had dragged the tigress into the river

bullet through its left eye, smashing open its skull. It was over in two seconds. The unfortunate crocodile opened its mouth and tried to groan. Its four feet flapped on the sand, and it died.

'The tigress, even quicker than me, had already removed her half-bitten paw from the mouth of her enemy.

'Louison's first reaction, I must say, did not suggest she had much confidence in me, or even that she was aware of what I had done. Perhaps she thought that she had as much to fear from me as from the crocodile. At first, she tried to run away, but the poor thing, reduced to three paws and almost crippled, could not go far. After ten paces, I caught up with her.

'I must tell you, Messieurs, that I already felt a great deal of friendly warmth towards her. First of all, I had rendered her a great service and, as you know, it is natural to attach yourself to someone whom you have helped, more than you do with someone who has helped you. Second, she seemed to have an excellent character, and even the prank she played on the crocodile suggested that she had a joyful spirit; and joy, as you know, Messieurs, when it is not false, is the sign of a good heart and a good conscience.

'I was alone, you see, in a strange country, five thousand leagues from Saint-Malo, without friends, without parents, without family. And it seemed to me that the friendship of someone who owed me their life – even if that friend had four paws, powerful claws and terrifying teeth – was worth a great deal more than nothing.

'Was I wrong?

'No, Messieurs, I wasn't – and what happened afterwards proved that.

'But I mustn't get ahead of myself, and I ought to say that

Louison didn't then appear to need a friend as much as I did.

'When I got close to her, I saw her in pain, only able to stand on three legs. Then she lay down on her back, and from that desperate position, seemed to await my attack. She let out a hoarse cry – which she always does when she's angry. She ground her teeth, flashed her claws and seemed ready to eat me, or at least to make sure that her life would only be lost at great cost to her attacker.

'But I know how to tame the wildest of beasts.

'I moved forward calmly. I put my rifle down on the sand, still close to me, and leant over the tigress and gently caressed her head as if she were a child.

'At first she looked at me sideways on, as if to question me. But when she saw that my intentions were good, she rolled on to her stomach, and gently licked my hand. With a sad look she presented me with her injured paw. And for my part, I felt the importance of that mark of confidence, and I looked at her paw with great care. Nothing was broken. The teeth of the crocodile had not penetrated deeply, largely because of the way in which Louison had sunk her claws into his tongue.

'I washed her wound carefully. I pulled out a flask of alkaline solution from my hunting bag, and put one or two drops on the wound. Then I signalled to Louison to follow me.

'I'm not sure whether it was because of some special understanding between us, or because she wanted me to bandage her, but she let me lead her to the carriage. The two Malays who were accompanying me almost died of fear when they saw Louison. They jumped out of the back of the carriage, and nothing would make them climb back in again.

'The following day we returned to Batavia. Cornelius van

I put two drops of alkaline solution on her wound

Crittenden was astonished to see me with my new friend, whom I had given the name Louison, and who followed me about the streets like a puppy.

'Eight days later I lifted anchor, having brought the tigress on board with me. She had never left my side since our first encounter. And that same night, not far from Borneo, she saved my life.

'My brig was taken by surprise in calm weather three leagues off the coast of Borneo. It was nearly midnight, and my crew, consisting of only twelve men, was sleeping. About a hundred Malay pirates boarded the ship at once, and threw the sailor who was at the helm into the sea.

'This act of murder was carried out so swiftly, with no one hearing the slightest noise, that it was impossible to protect the unfortunate sailor.

'Then the pirates began trying to break down the door of my cabin. But Louison was asleep inside, at the foot of my bed. She was woken by the noise, and began to growl in a terrifying manner. And in a couple of seconds I was upright, a pistol in each hand, and a small hatchet between my teeth.

'At that very moment, the pirates broke through the door and entered my cabin. The first of them had his brains blown away with a pistol shot. The second also fell to a bullet. The third was thrown to the ground by Louison who, with one bite, broke his neck. With a blow of my hatchet, I split open the head of a fourth pirate, and I went to the bridge to get the help of my sailors.

'Throughout this time, Louison was wonderful. With one leap, she knocked over three pirates who were trying to follow me. With another leap, she landed in the middle of a skirmish. She seemed to move at the speed of light.

'Two minutes later she had killed six pirates. Each of her claws was like the point of a sword entering the skin of these unfortunates. Even though she suffered three injuries and lost some blood, this only seemed to make her more ardent in battle, and more willing to protect me with her body.

'At last my sailors arrived, armed with revolvers and iron bars. From that point on, victory was ours. About twenty of the pirates were thrown into the sea, the others jumped overboard, and tried to swim for their boats. We lost only one man, the one whose throat had been cut at the beginning.

'As you can imagine, I bandaged Louison with great care. Since that night, when she paid off her debt, I vowed that nothing will ever separate us, until death. We will never leave each other.

'Messieurs, I beg your pardon for the liberties I took in bringing Louison here. I left her in the antechamber, but the porter saw her, became frightened, locked the door, and sounded the alarm – as a means of rescuing you.'

'Well, Monsieur,' said the Presiding Officer softly, 'whether it is your fault, or that of Mademoiselle Louison, or of the porter, we have spent an afternoon in the company of a ferocious beast, and for this reason our dinner will be quite cold.'

At this point, the Presiding Officer of the Academy of Sciences (of Lyon) was interrupted by a loud noise. The beating of drums could be heard, and there was much peering out of the windows to see what was happening.

'The Lord be praised!' said the Secretary-for-Life, 'we will soon be rescued.'

The Commissioner of Police stepped forward

And, indeed, three thousand people filled the square outside and the nearby streets. A company of infantrymen was in the vanguard, and they were aiming their rifles at the Academy building.

Then the Commissioner of Police, wearing a sash in the colours of the French flag, stepped forward, signalled the drums to be silent, and said, in a commanding voice, 'In the name of the law, give yourselves up!'

'Commissioner,' shouted the Presiding Officer from the window, 'it's not a question of us giving ourselves up, but of just opening the door.'

The Commissioner of Police, who had taken the precaution of bringing along several locksmiths, ordered the removal of all the obstacles which had been placed outside the door of the Academy to block Louison's passage.

When his orders had been executed, the commanding officer of the infantry regiment shouted, 'Prepare arms! Take aim!'

They were getting ready to shoot Louison the moment she appeared.

'Messieurs,' said Corcoran to the academicians, 'you can leave. When you are safe, I will leave the building, and Louison will only leave at my side. Don't be scared.'

'Captain, make sure you do nothing imprudent,' said the Presiding Officer as he shook Corcoran's hand and said goodbye.

The academicians left as quickly as they could. Louison watched them with a look of astonishment, and seemed keen to follow in their footsteps, but Corcoran held her back.

When the two of them were alone in the building, Corcoran

gestured to Louison to return to the assembly room while he stepped out on to the porch to speak to the Commissioner of Police.

'Commissioner,' he said, 'I am ready to bring my tiger out peacefully, if you promise to do her no harm. We will go straight to the steamboat waiting on the River Rhône, and I promise to keep Louison in my cabin so that no one will be disturbed or frightened.'

'No, no! Death to the tiger!' screamed the crowd, which was excited about the thought of seeing a tiger hunt.

'Step aside, Monsieur,' shouted the Commissioner of Police.

Corcoran made one more attempt to convince him, but nothing could persuade this inflexible official to change his mind.

Then the man from Saint-Malo appeared to give in. He beckoned Louison, and bending down he hugged her tenderly. He may have whispered something in her ear.

'Now,' said the Commissioner of Police, 'that's enough of all that.'

Corcoran looked around with an air of dismay.

'I am ready,' he said finally, 'but please don't shoot until I am out of the door. I do not wish to witness the murder of my closest friend before my very eyes.'

This request was thought reasonable, and Corcoran was allowed to come down the stairs. Louison, lurking behind the open door of the assembly room, watched Corcoran leave, but kept her head low. She seemed to suspect the dangers that threatened her. It was a moment of fearful expectation.

Suddenly Corcoran, who had already got past the company

of infantry, turned round and shouted three times, 'Louison! Louison! Louison!'

On hearing this cry, this signal, the tiger made a terrifying leap and landed at the bottom of the stairs.

Before the officer could order his troops to fire, Louison took another great leap above the heads of the soldiers, and began to run towards Captain Corcoran.

'Shoot! Shoot!' shouted the horrified crowd.

But the officer ordered his troops to hold fire. In order to shoot the tiger, one might have killed or wounded fifty people in the crowd. Instead, the soldiers had to content themselves with following Corcoran and Louison to the port, where the two of them embarked peacefully, as the captain had promised.

The following day, Captain Corcoran arrived in Marseilles and awaited the instructions of the Academy of Sciences of Lyon. These instructions, written by the Secretary-for-Life himself, were composed in a manner that would make them worthy of being entered into the annals of history. But an unfortunate incident would later force the Captain to throw them into the fire, and so one is reduced to guessing their contents from the rest of the story of the celebrated Captain from Saint-Malo. But it may suffice to say that they were worthy of the learned society which sent them and of the illustrious traveller to whom they were sent.

4

Louison and Corcoran encounter an Indian princess

Calcutta

1st January 1857

Lord Henry Braddock, Governor-General of Hindustan[12] *to Colonel Barclay, Resident at the court of Holkar, Prince of the Marathas, Bhagavpur on the Narmada River*[13]

I am reliably informed, by various sources, that something is brewing. The natives have been sending mysterious signals to each other in Lucknow, Patna, Benares, Delhi and among the Rajputs and even among the Sikhs.

If some kind of revolt breaks out and reaches the lands of the Marathas, all of India will be on fire in the space of three weeks. Everything possible must be done to stop this.

As soon as you receive this letter, you should therefore make sure, under whatever pretext, that Holkar disarms his fortresses, and hands over to us all his cannons, his guns, his ammunition and his treasure. In that way, he will not be able to cause trouble, and his treasure will serve as a hostage should he, in spite of these precautions, wish to embark on some desperate attempt at rebellion against us. And in truth, the coffers of the East India Company[14] are empty, and his money would be most welcome.

If he refuses, it is because he has evil intentions towards us, and in that case he does not deserve to be pardoned. You will take immediate command of the 13th, 15th and 31st regiments of European infantry, which Sir William Maxwell, the Governor of Bombay, will put under your orders along with four or five regiments of native cavalry and infantry. You will place Bhagavpur under siege, and it is up to you to decide the conditions under which Holkar will be allowed to surrender. The best situation is if Holkar is killed in the siege, like Tippoo Sahib,[15] because the East India Company has had enough of rebellious vassals, and we would, thereby, be saved the bother of providing a lifelong pension to those who detest us.

I leave the rest to your discretion, but move quickly, because there is a growing fear of some kind of eruption, and we must make sure that the rebels (if there is to be a rebellion) have no leaders and no weapons.

Braddock
Governor-General

Bhagavpur
18th January 1857

Colonel Barclay, English Resident, to Prince Holkar

The undersigned has the duty of advising His Highness Prince Holkar that it has come to his notice that the said Prince struck his Prime Minister, Rao, fifty times with a stick. There is no reason known to the undersigned which would explain such cruel treatment.

The undersigned also advises His Highness that on several occasions recently heavily laden carts have entered the fortress of Bhagavpur during the night. According to a variety of sources, about whom I need say no more, they were carrying weapons, supplies and ammunitions. This is contrary to our treaty, and will only arouse the justified suspicion of the most-exalted and most-powerful East India Company.

In consequence, and after having received my orders from the Governor-General, the undersigned – without wishing to deprive Prince Holkar of that authority which is anyway so widely opposed in his own land – the undersigned would like on this occasion to close his ears to the stories being told by our faithful friends, and instead offer Prince Holkar the clear opportunity of justifying himself. The undersigned is content, for now, to ask that His Highness put all his weapons, cannons, rifles and his personal treasury in the hands of the undersigned, who will send them to Calcutta, where the Governor-General will take provisional charge of them, until there is definitive proof of the innocence of Holkar.

Furthermore, the said Prince Holkar is invited to put into the care of the undersigned his only daughter Sita, who will be taken to Calcutta with her retinue, and who will receive all the honours appropriate to her rank.

In return, His Highness is assured of the eternal and benevolent protection of the most-exalted and most-powerful East India Company.

Colonel Barclay

Prince Holkar to Colonel Barclay, Resident

The undersigned has made it his duty to invite Colonel Barclay to leave Bhagavpur immediately, failing which he will have his head chopped off within twenty-four hours by the order of the undersigned.

Holkar

Colonel Barclay to Lord Henry Braddock, Governor-General

My Lord,

I have the honour of sending to your Lordship a copy of the letter which I, following your instructions, wrote to Prince Holkar along with the response of the said Holkar. I am now leaving for Bombay, where I will, in accordance with your Lordship's order, take command of the army corps with which I will bring Holkar to reason.

I am, Sir, your most obedient, etc....

Colonel Barclay

About six weeks after this exchange of letters, Holkar was sitting, wrapped in thought, on a Persian carpet, at the top of the highest tower in his palace on the banks of the Narmada

Holkar was sitting on a Persian carpet

River. He was looking out, in a melancholy manner, at the high peaks of the ancient Vindhya Mountains, as old as Brahma himself. Next to him sat his only daughter, the beautiful Sita, who was looking at her father, trying to read his thoughts.

Holkar was an old nobleman, a pure Indian and the descendant of the Maratha princes who had fought the English for the control of India.

His ancestors were a rare exception in that they had not been conquered by the Persians or the Mughals, and were able, well-guarded by the mountains, to continue to worship Brahma. Holkar himself was directly descended from the celebrated Rama, the most illustrious of ancient heroes, who defeated the demon Ravana. It was in honour of these glorious origins that he gave his daughter the name of Rama's wife, Sita.

Holkar had fought the British before. His father had been killed in battle, and he, still a youngster, was allowed to keep his kingdom so long as he paid tribute to the British. For thirty years he had hoped that one day he would get his vengeance. But his beard had turned white, his two sons had died without an heir, and he now only dreamed of living in peace, and bequeathing his kingdom to his only daughter, the beautiful Sita.

It was about five o'clock in the evening. All was quiet in Bhagavpur, Holkar's capital. The watchmen were at their posts, their eyes fixed on the horizon. Some of the soldiers were crouching on their heels, playing chess, not saying a word. A few officers on horseback, armed with long scimitars, trotted through the streets to keep everything in order. As they passed by, everyone fell silent. A deathly sadness seemed to have invaded Bhagavpur.

Holkar himself was downcast, defeated. He could see the coming storm. He had known for a long time that the English would eventually destroy him, and he despaired when he thought of the future for his daughter. For himself, Holkar was resigned to the will of Brahma, ready to return to what he called 'the Great Being', and to find the 'Eternal Substance'. But he could not bear to leave Sita defenceless, without protection.

'Let the will of Brahma be done!' he said in answer to his innermost thoughts.

'My father,' said the beautiful Sita, 'what are you dreaming about?'

One could search in vain throughout all of India, from Cape Comorin in the south to the Himalayas in the north, for a young woman as charming as Sita. She stood as straight as a palm tree and her eyes were like lotus flowers. She was hardly fifteen years old, and that, in India, is the age of greatest beauty.

'I was thinking,' said Holkar, 'that cursed was the day on which I saw your birth; yes, you, the joy of my eyes, my last earthly love, because when I die you will fall into the hands of these red-coated barbarians.'

'But,' asked Sita, 'is there really no chance of victory?'

'If I had the slightest hope, don't you think I would be out there, encouraging my soldiers? But I can only think of these impure men, who feast on our sacred cows, who live off raw meat and blood, to the horror of our priests. Ah, why did I not perish alongside the last of my sons? I should not have to see the ruin of all that is dear to me.'

'Don't forget me,' said Sita, getting up and putting her arms around the neck of the old man.

'I've not forgotten you, my dear daughter, but I fear for

you; while for your brothers I only had death to fear. I've just learnt that Colonel Barclay and his army are advancing on the Narmada Valley. He's only seven leagues from here, about two days' march. Because that ponderous race of people always brings so many animals, carriages, cannons and ammunition of all kinds it can never travel more than two or three leagues in a day. Unfortunately, I don't dare take the fight to them by the riverside because I am not sure of my army. I suspect that miserable Rao of wanting to betray me. If I could prove it, that miserable man would pay dearly for his treason.

'But,' he continued, looking at the horizon through his telescope, 'what is that steamer doing at the bend of the river? Surely Barclay's vanguard can't already be so close.'

At that moment, there was the sound of cannon fire. An artilleryman in the fortress had fired at the steamboat, as a way of ordering it to stop. The cannonball flew over the boat and landed, with a whistling sound, in the river.

In response, the captain of the steamboat hoisted the French flag and, without firing back, steered towards the riverbank. The astonished Indians did not attempt to stop the boat from landing, and Captain Corcoran (for it was he) stepped out on to the riverbank and began walking with an air of confidence towards the fort. A sergeant and several soldiers were planning to cross bayonets and bar his passage, but Corcoran, without responding to their questions and their threats (though he understood their language perfectly) turned round slowly and looked in the direction of the boat. He took the whistle that was hanging from his belt and put it to his lips.

The screech of the whistle was as sharp as the point of a sword, and all the Prince's men shivered. Their shivering became

Captain Corcoran arrives in Bhagavpur

terror when they saw a magnificent tigress standing on the prow of the boat, responding to the whistle with a formidable roar.

'Here, Louison,' shouted Corcoran.

And he blew his whistle a second time.

Louison responded by leaping from the steamboat, already moored, to the riverbank. One minute later, all the officers, the soldiers, the gunners, the infantrymen, the curious and ordinary men and women, and their little children had run away in every direction. Except for the unfortunate commander of the watch, who had fired the cannon at the steamboat a little earlier, and whom Captain Corcoran had just seized by his neck.

'Let me go,' said the Indian, who fought back with all his strength, 'let me go or I will call the guard.'

'If you,' said Corcoran, 'make the slightest move without my permission, I will hand you over to Louison for her dinner.'

This threat made the poor officer more docile than a lamb.

'Alas, all-powerful Lord, whom I do not know, hold back your tigress, or I will be a dead man.'

Louison, deprived of fresh meat for a long time, walked round the Indian with a famished look on her face. She found him very appetising, not too young, not too old, not too fat, not too thin, but tender and plump – a perfect meal.

Fortunately, Corcoran was able to reassure the officer.

'What is your rank?' he asked

'Lieutenant, your Lordship,' replied the Indian.

'Take me to the palace of Prince Holkar.'

'With your… friend?' asked the Indian, hesitating.

'By Jove,' replied Corcoran. 'Do you think I'm ashamed of my friends when I go to court?'

'O, Brahma and Buddha!' thought the poor Indian. 'What a stupid idea of mine to fire a cannonball at that steamboat which was causing no harm at all. O Rama, invincible hero, lend me your strength and your bow so that my arrows can pierce Louison. Or lend me your great agility so that I can take to my heels, and find safety in my home.'

'Very good,' said Corcoran, 'have you finished your meditations now? Louison is getting impatient.'

'But my Lord,' replied the Indian, 'if I take you to the palace of Prince Holkar with a tigress at your heels, or rather mine – Holkar will cut off your head.'

'You think so?' asked Corcoran.

'Do I think so? Yes, I do, my Lord. I do. Prince Holkar never performs his evening prayers unless he has had five or six people impaled during the day.'

'Ah, I rather like this Holkar… I've decided: we will see if he impales me, or I impale him.'

'But my Lord, he will undoubtedly start with me.'

'Enough excuses. Start walking, or I will get Louison to encourage you.'

This threat gave the Indian some courage. After all, he wasn't absolutely sure that Holkar would impale him, whilst he was just six inches away from the teeth and claws of Louison.

He said a final silent prayer to Brahma, 'Father of all Beings', and walked rapidly towards the entrance to the palace. Corcoran followed closely behind, and Louison, full of joy, leapt around next to her master like an overfriendly hunting dog.

Thanks to his double escort, Corcoran had no trouble entering the palace. Everyone moved out of their way. But when they arrived at the foot of the tower where Prince Holkar was sitting with his daughter, their Indian escort refused to go further.

'My Lord,' he said, 'if I go up there with you, my death is certain. Before I would have a chance to say a single word to justify myself, Holkar would cut off my head. And yourself, my Lord, if you persist with this foolish course of action, you will…'

'Enough, enough,' replied Corcoran. 'Holkar isn't as evil as they say, I'm sure of that. And he won't refuse anything to my friend Louison. As for you, that's another matter. Be away with you, coward.'

'My Lord,' the Indian said humbly, 'there's no head that would fit better on my shoulders than my own; and if it pleased the great prince to remove it there is no ointment in the world that could stick it back on again. Brahma and Buddha be with you!'

And then he ran away.

Corcoran made no attempt to bring him back, and instead climbed, without stopping, the two hundred and sixty steps which led to the terrace from where Prince Holkar silently contemplated the Narmada Valley.

Louison went ahead of her master, and was the first to reach the terrace.

On seeing the tigress, Sita let out a cry of fear, and Prince Holkar got up hurriedly, pulling a pistol from his belt and firing it at Louison. Fortunately, the bullet hit the wall, and then ricocheted into Corcoran, who was following closely behind his friend, causing a slight injury to his hand.

'You are a lively fellow, Lord Holkar,' shouted the Captain, without showing any surprise about being hurt. 'Come here, Louison!'

It was time to hold back the tigress, who was about to leap on Prince Holkar and tear him to pieces.

'Here, my child,' continued Corcoran. 'There, that's good. Sit at my feet. Very good. And now, go and crawl up to the Princess and pay your respects. You have nothing to fear, Madame. Louison is as docile as a lamb. She's asking your pardon for having frightened you. Go Louison, go my darling, ask the Princess to pardon you.'

Louison obeyed, and Sita, reassured, stroked her gently, which seemed to please the tigress greatly.

However, Holkar was still on the defensive.

'Who are you?' he asked haughtily. 'How did you manage to get in here? Have I already been betrayed by my own servants and handed over to the English?'

'My Lord,' replied Corcoran softly, 'you have not been betrayed. If there is one thing to thank God for, after he had the goodness to make me a Breton called Corcoran, it is that he did not make me an Englishman.'

Holkar, without responding to him, picked up a small silver hammer and used it to bang a large gong.

Nobody appeared.

'My Lord Holkar,' said Corcoran with a smile, 'no one can hear you. When they saw Louison, they all ran away. But be assured, Louison is a well-brought-up girl, and knows how to behave herself. And now, my Lord, what is this treason that you fear?'

'If you are not English,' replied Holkar, 'then who are you and where do you come from?'

'My Lord,' said Corcoran, 'there are, in this vast universe, two sorts of men – or, if you want, two principal races, not including yours. They are the French and the English, who are to each other as the dog is to the wolf, or the tiger to the buffalo, or the panther to the rattlesnake. Each of these pairings is hungry – the one for praise, the other for money – but they are equally quarrelsome, and always ready to meddle in the affairs of the other without being invited. I belong to the first of these two races. I am Captain Corcoran…'

'What?' said Holkar 'you are the famous captain who commanded the brig called *The Son of the Tempest*?'

'Famous or not,' said the Breton, 'I am the same Captain Corcoran.'

'And it's you,' asked Holkar, 'who, when surprised by two hundred Malay pirates near Singapore, with your seven soldiers, threw the pirates into the sea?'

'That's me,' said Corcoran. 'Where did you read about this?'

'In the *Bombay Times*. But those English rogues always say that they rule the oceans, and led us to believe that Corcoran was an Englishman.'

'An Englishman? Me?' the Captain cried out indignantly.

'Yes, but the error didn't survive uncorrected. A dozen of the pirates, as you will know, were hanged, but a thirteenth escaped while he was being taken to the gallows. He slipped away into the backstreets of Singapore, where he hid for some time, until he was able to get on board a Chinese boat, from where he came to Calcutta, and from Calcutta he came here in search of asylum. He's an Indian Muslim. And he's the one who told me about you. He's around here somewhere.'

Just then a servant appeared on the threshold of the terrace. He was quite tall, well built and handsome in the European manner, though his limbs were a little spindly, as if he had greater agility than strength.

On seeing Corcoran, and especially Louison, he howled out loud and got ready to flee, but Holkar called him over.

'Ali!' he said.

'My Lord.'

'Look carefully at this white-skinned foreigner. Do you know him?'

Ali advanced uncertainly, but he had hardly looked at Corcoran when he shouted out, 'Master, it's him!'

'Who?'

'The Captain. And that's her,' he added on seeing the tigress. 'My Lord, my Lord, please protect me.'

'Excellent,' said the Captain, merrily. 'Do you think we bear grudges? Go, brave man! You should have been hanged, but you managed to avoid the coiled rope being tightened around your neck. I don't blame you for that, and Prince Holkar has done well to take you into his service – that is, if he doesn't mind the company of brigands.'

'But,' said Holkar, turning to Ali, 'why is there such commotion in the streets of Bhagavpur. What are those screams, and that gunfire, and the beating drums?'

'My Lord,' said Ali, 'I came here to warn you about this. When Captain Corcoran set foot on land, it was thought that he had been sent by the English. Your former minister Rao spread the rumour that you had been killed by a pistol shot and that the English army was just two leagues from the city. Some of the troops are supporting him, and he's boasting of his right to your crown.'

'Ah, that traitor!' said Holkar. 'I will have him impaled.'

'He says he has the support of the English, and he's begun to lay siege to the palace.'

'Ah-ha,' said Corcoran, 'this situation is becoming interesting.'

Until then the beautiful Sita had remained totally silent, but on realizing the danger for her father, she leapt forward, facing Captain Corcoran, and grasped his hands.

'My Lord,' she said, crying, 'please save him!'

'Gadzooks!' said Corcoran. 'Let it never be said that Captain Corcoran was immune to the tears and the prayers of a woman with such beautiful eyes. Lord Holkar, can you give me a revolver and a whip? With them in my hands, I can sort all this out and, more particularly, deal with that traitor Rao'.

Ali hurriedly brought him both weapons. Then the Prince, Corcoran and Ali went down the stairs, while the beautiful Sita, now prostrate on the ground, called on Brahma to protect her defenders.

A small number of guards still controlled the main gateway to the palace, though they seemed on the point of surrendering to the crowd which had gathered outside. Three regiments of rebellious soldiers were attacking the gates and shouting seditious slogans. Rao, on horseback, was in command, and encouraging the attack. Bullets were whistling past in all directions, and the rebels were bringing cannons to break down the gates. Corcoran knew there was not a minute to lose.

'Open the gates,' he said, 'I'll deal with them all.'

The Captain's air of assurance gave his host confidence. Holkar ordered the gates to be opened, and this action so astonished the soldiers, who feared some kind of trap, that they pulled back instinctively. The firing stopped and a great silence fell.

'Where is Lord Rao?' Corcoran asked in a forceful voice.

'I'm here,' replied Rao, who approached on his horse, followed by his officers. 'Is Holkar ready to surrender?'

'By Jove,' said Corcoran, 'what an impudent joker!'

Corcoran whistled gently.

On hearing the whistle, Louison appeared.

'My dear,' said Corcoran, 'go and fetch me that rascal on horseback. Don't hurt him. Carry him carefully between your teeth, without breaking or tearing anything, and bring him to me… Did you hear me, my dear?'

And he gestured in the direction of the unfortunate Rao, who attempted to ride away. But regrettably for him, his horse reared up and began to kick in the air. The other horses were no calmer, and their riders turned and galloped in disarray through the lines of infantry, afraid of being mistaken for Rao by Louison.

Rao would have liked to follow their example, but fate had other plans. Louison had already leapt on to the hindquarters of his horse. She seized the unfortunate Rao by his waist and jumped to the ground. Then, like a cat with a mouse between its teeth who does not want to kill its victim immediately, she deposited the half-conscious Rao at the feet of the Captain.

'That's good, my child,' said Corcoran affectionately. 'You will have sugar for supper. Ali, disarm that old rogue and keep him prisoner, while I talk to these other imbeciles.'

Then, advancing, whip in hand, he stood within five paces of the first line of soldiers, whose rifles were loaded and ready to fire.

She seized the unfortunate Rao by his waist

'Would any of you,' he asked, 'like to be hanged or impaled or decapitated or burnt alive, or handed over to Louison? Ah, no response?'

They were all terrified. Captain Corcoran, who seemed to have fallen from the sky, astonished the superstitious Indians. The claws and teeth of Louison scared them still more. And, after all, why should they rebel now that Rao was in the hands of Holkar?

Suddenly everyone began to shout, 'Long live Prince Holkar.'

'That's better!' said Corcoran. 'I see that you have decided to stay loyal to your legitimate prince, after all. Now disarm the three colonels, the three lieutenant colonels and the three majors.

'That's right, tie up their hands and feet and make them lie down on the ground... That's perfect. And you, my boys, return peacefully to your barracks, and if I hear a murmur from anyone, Louison will eat him for dinner. Goodnight then, and now Lord Holkar, let us have our supper.'

5

A secret messenger reaches Bhagavpur

Under the starry skies, in an inner courtyard of the palace, a dinner table had been laid next to a fountain of water. Prince Holkar, his lotus-eyed daughter and Captain Corcoran were seated in the European style – that is, on chairs – and there were about twenty servants looking after them. The diners ate in silence, a mark of gravitas among Asian royalty.

Next to them, Louison, lying between her master and the beautiful Sita, was fed alternately by each of them, and responded by giving them tender looks.

Sita, in recognition of the service rendered by Louison and pleased by her obedience, treated the tigress like a favourite hunting dog, lavishing her with sugar and flattery. While Louison, too intelligent not to understand Sita's good intentions, wagged her tail as a way of thanking her and stretched out her long neck, so that the young woman could stroke the head of her new friend.

Then Holkar gestured for his servants to retire and leave him alone with his daughter and Corcoran.

'Captain,' said Holkar, shaking his hand, 'you've just saved my life and my throne. How can I show my gratitude?'

Corcoran raised his head with a look of mild astonishment.

'Lord Holkar,' he said, 'the service I have rendered you was such a little thing that in truth it would be better if you and I spoke no more about it. Anyway, it was mainly thanks to Louison, who showed such tact and discretion in this whole matter that I can't praise her enough. She hadn't eaten well. She was hungry. She was in a bad mood. You had just shot at her with your pistol… I don't reproach you for that. It was the result of a most excusable error… And you missed. She might well have made a small meal out of you at that point. But she controlled her appetite, repressed her natural instincts. And that's a lot, if you think about the pretty basic education she had in the forests of Java. In the meantime, a rascal stirs up discontent among your soldiers – which, between you and me, doesn't appear to be a very hard thing to do – and then gets them to rebel against you. And if you had stepped outside the walls of your palace, you would have had your throat cut like a chicken. But Louison knew what to do. She seized the unfortunate Rao by his backside (Alas! I fear he will never be able to sit down again) and deposited him at your feet. Frankly, if you have anyone to thank, it's Louison. As for me, I just followed in her footsteps.'

'My Lord Corcoran,' said the beautiful Sita, 'I owe you my life and my honour. I will never forget that.'

She held out her hand to the Captain, who kissed it respectfully.

'I realise, Captain,' said Holkar, 'that you come from a generous nation, and do not want payment for your services, but is there any way I can be useful to you?'

'Useful, dear Prince?' exclaimed Corcoran. 'You may be more than useful to me... Did you know that I have come to India in search of an old manuscript, the very thought of which makes all the learned people of France and England quiver with pleasure? Did you know that the Academy of Sciences of Lyon has paid the costs of my voyage? So Louison and I are travelling in the interests of science, and under the protection of the French government. We also have letters of recommendation for all the high officials of the English government in India. And I have a letter for you from the illustrious Sir William Barrowlinson, president of the Geographical, Colonial, Statistical, Geological, Orographical, Hydrographical and Photographical Society, based in London, in Oxford Street, number 183. Here it is.'

And from his pocketbook, he pulled out a letter with a large red seal, and decorated with the crest and motto of the learned baronet, which dates back (of that he's certain) to his ancestor, a companion in arms of William the Conqueror: *Regi meo fidus*.

(And, in fact, Sir William Barrowlinson had a thousand reasons to be, in the words of his motto, 'faithful to his king', because the said king had made the said Barrowlinson, at the age of twenty, one of the most important directors of the East India Company. And he had accumulated so many honorary positions, and so many important designations, that – but for a most regrettable gastric problem – he would have become, at the age of thirty-two or thirty-three, the Viceroy of India,[16] that's to say the almost absolute master of one hundred million people. His gastric problem forced him to return to England, where he lived off an annual pension of three hundred thousand francs. This meant that he could become a Member of Parliament, do a fairly good translation of fifteen or eighteen pages of the Vedas, and hire an assistant to continue the translation in his name. He also agreed to preside over the Geographical, Colonial, Statistical, Orographical, Hydrographical and Photographical Society, and become Corresponding Member of the Institute of France.)

It was from this powerful individual that the letter of recommendation that Captain Corcoran presented to Prince Holkar had come.

> The undersigned, Sir William Barrowlinson, has the honour of advising His Highness Prince Holkar of the journey of the young French scholar, Monsieur Corcoran, who proposes, under the guidance of the Academy of Sciences of Lyon, and of our own learned societies, to find the original manuscript of the *Ramabagavattana.*[17] The manuscript is thought to have been deposited, as Your Highness Prince Holkar knows better than anyone (or at least that's the opinion of the undersigned), somewhere near the source of the Narmada River.
>
> The undersigned is bold enough to boast that – in view of the close friendship and good neighbourly feeling that has always existed and which has not ceased to exist (at least that is the firm hope of the undersigned) between his Serene Highness Prince Holkar and the most-exalted, most-sublime, most-powerful and most-invincible East India Company – he believes that His Highness will endeavour to assist, by all means possible, the scientific research with which Captain

Corcoran has been charged by the Academy of Sciences of Lyon, and with the authorisation of Her Most Gracious and Most Noble Majesty, Victoria, first of that name, and sovereign of the three united kingdoms of England, Scotland and Ireland.

To that end, the undersigned, Sir William Barrowlinson, President of the Geographical, Colonial, Statistical, Geological, Orographical, Hydrographical and Photographical Society, has the duty of asking His Serene Highness to put at the disposition of the said captain all the necessary resources: be they camels, elephants, palanquins, labourers, horsemen, foot soldiers and in general all that he believes he needs for his expedition. And the said Sir William Barrowlinson pledges in his own name and that of the Academy of Sciences of Lyon to cover all expenses incurred, and reimburse His Highness, if he is so willing, for any sums he provides to this young and learned traveller.

Furthermore, the undersigned should advise His Highness that the mission of Captain Corcoran (he has given his word of honour) is and should remain strictly non-political.

Finally, the undersigned trusts that the gentleman whom he respectfully asks permission to present to His Highness, will honour in every way the noble nation of which he is a citizen, the glorious nation which protects him, the scientific endeavour which he serves, the illustrious and learned society which sends him, and the undersigned who recommends him.

It is with these sentiments that the undersigned respectfully and affectionately remembers His Highness, hoping that time has not lessened the friendship which Prince Holkar had shown towards him in the past, and which the undersigned has kept and will continue to keep in his heart as a most grateful memory.

Sir William Barrowlinson, Baronet, MP

Once Prince Holkar had finished reading, he held out his hand to Corcoran and said:

'My dear friend, between us there is no need of such letters. And because I am on such poor terms with the English, this one from Sir William Barrowlinson would not have helped you, if I had not otherwise known who you are, and if I hadn't witnessed the courage with which you saved my life. Unfortunately, Colonel Barclay is, I know for certain, marching on Bhagavpur, and even if I hadn't known it, Rao's treason would have taught me about it this very evening. But I am not sure I will be able to help you with your quest. And I fear that my friendship with you will harm you in the eyes of the English.'

'Lord Holkar,' said the Captain, 'don't worry about me and the English. If Colonel Barclay doesn't treat me as a friend, he will soon learn, even if he has thirty regiments, the full weight of my fist as I strike him. So don't have any worries about me; and perhaps, on the contrary, I can serve you, and help bring about peace.'

'Make peace with those barbarians!' exclaimed Holkar, his eyes glowing with fury. 'They killed my father and my two brothers; they have taken half my land and pillaged the other half. By the resplendent Indra, whose chariot crosses the heavens and brings light to the most obscure parts of the universe, if I could give all my treasure and my life to throw the last of these red-coated barbarians into the sea, I would not hesitate for a moment. Yes, I swear I would, today if I could, and then happily join my ancestors in the Eternal and Incorruptible Substance.'

'And you would leave me all alone on earth,' interrupted the beautiful Sita with a voice of soft reproach.

'Oh, I am sorry, my sweet child,' said the old man hugging his daughter to his chest. 'Just the mention of the English fills me with horror. Please forgive me, Captain...'

'Forgiven, my dear host,' said Corcoran, 'and don't be embarrassed about cursing the English. For me, apart from Sir William Barrowlinson, who seems to be a good man, even if he can be a little long-winded, I care no more for the English than I would for a sour herring or a sardine in oil. I am a Breton, and a sailor – and that says it all. Between the Anglo-Saxon race and me there is little love lost.'

'You've made me happy, Captain,' said Holkar, 'at first, I feared that you were a friend of theirs. And when I think of the future they intend for my poor Sita, my blood boils with fury in my old veins, and I would like to chop off the heads of all the English who are in India. But let's talk no more of this. And you, my dear Sita, to calm me down after that outburst, please read some passages to me from one of those beautiful books which celebrate the glory of our ancestors.'

'Would you like me to read,' said Sita, 'that passage from the *Ramayana*, the touching one about the sadness of King Dasharatha on his deathbed, mourning the fact that his dear son, Rama, the great hero, is not with him? And how he accused himself of having deserved this punishment from the gods, because he had accidentally committed a murder when he was a young man.'

'Good. Yes, read!' replied Holkar.

Sita got up, quickly found the book and began to read.

I arrived beside the deserted banks of the river Sarayu, when I was seized by the desire to shoot an animal with my bow, but to do so without looking, by sound alone, something I had practised many times. So I hid myself in the shadows, my bow at the ready, close to the watering-hole where the beasts of the forest come at night to slake their thirst.

Then I heard the sound of a jug being filled with water, so similar to the murmurings of an elephant. I immediately placed a well-feathered arrow in my bow and fired it in the direction from which the sound was coming.

At the very moment when the arrow reached its target, I heard the voice of a man, crying out loud, in the saddest of tones. 'Ah, I am dead. How could anyone fire an arrow at a holy man like me? Who could have so cruel a hand as to direct an arrow at me? I came alone to the river at night to fetch some water. So whom could I have offended?'

This was what he said, and on hearing these sad words, my soul was troubled and I trembled with fear because of the mistake I had made, and I let the weapons I was carrying fall to the ground. I headed towards him, and I saw, fallen in the water, pierced through the heart, an unfortunate young man clothed in an antelope skin.

He was deeply wounded and stared at me as if he wanted to burn me up in the fires of his radiant saintliness.

'O warrior, what harm have I done to you,' he said, 'alone as I was, living in the woods, that I deserved to be shot with an arrow, when I only wanted to fetch water for my parents? Those old authors of my existence are waiting for me now, two poor blind people, without support in the empty forest, hoping for my return. You have killed with that one arrow three people at the same time: my father, my mother and me. For what reason?

'Go quickly, son of Raghu, go and find my parents and tell them about this fatal event, so that you will not be consumed by a curse, in the way that fire consumes dry wood. This path that you see leads to my father's hermitage. Go there quickly, but first pull out this arrow.'

So that was how the young man spoke to me. In his view, I had fallen extremely low.

And so, reluctantly, I removed the arrow that had pierced the breast of this young hermit, with the utmost care, in view of my great desire to keep him alive. But hardly had I pulled out the arrow than this son of hermits, exhausted by suffering, and whose breathing was like the sound of heavy sobbing, went into convulsions, rolled his eyes and drew his final breath.

I took his jug, and headed towards his father's hermitage.

There I saw both his parents: sad old people and blind, having no one to look after them, like two birds whose wings had been cut. They were seated, these distressed old people, longing for their son, talking to each other about him.

When they heard my footsteps, the old man spoke to me, 'Why have you taken so long, my son? Your good mother and I were upset that you were absent for so long. If I, or your mother, have done something to displease you, pardon us – but do not leave us for so long. You are my legs, since I cannot walk; you are my eyes, since I cannot see. But why do you not speak to me?'

With these words, I approached the old man, my hands

joined together, sobs coming from my throat, trembling and feeling so much terror that I could only stammer.

'I am a warrior,' I said to him. 'I am known as Dasharatha, I am not your son. I have come here to you because I have committed a terrible crime.' And I told him about the murder of the young hermit.

On hearing these words the old man froze for a few moments, and when he had recovered his senses, he said, 'If, having committed such a sin, you hadn't confessed it to me spontaneously, then your entire people would have been punished, and I would have tormented them with a curse of fire. This crime will make Brahma get up from his throne. In your family, paradise will be closed to seven of your descendants, and seven of your ancestors.

'But you fired your arrow without knowing what you were doing, and it is because of that that you have not ceased to exist. Let us go, cruel one. Take me to the place where your arrow killed my child, where you broke the stick on which this blind man depends.'

So, on my own, I led the two blind parents to their son's place of death, and helped the hermit and his wife to feel his prostrate body.

Unable to bear the weight of their sorrow, they had barely touched the hand of their son when they both began to cry in pain, and they fell on his body that I had laid out on the ground. The mother, kissing the pallid face of her child, began to moan like a cow who has just been torn away from her young calf.

'Yajnadatta,' she said, 'are you not more precious than life? How can you not speak to me at this moment when you are leaving, hallowed child, for such a long voyage? Give your mother a kiss now, and you may leave after you have embraced me. Are you angry with me, is that why you don't speak?'

And the father, distressed and sick from pain, touched his son's cold limbs as if he were still alive, and spoke to his dead child with these moving words, 'My son, do you not recognise your father, who has come here with your mother? Get up, now. Come, reunite us by putting your arms round our necks. Who will now bring us wood and roots and wild fruit? And, my son, what about this repentant blind woman, your mother, bent by her years? Who will feed her? I am just as blind as she.

'We do not wish you to go away from us again. So tomorrow you will leave, my son, with your mother and me.'

At this point, Sita stopped reading. Holkar had been listening pensively. Even Corcoran was moved and looked at the soft and charming face of the young woman with admiration.

It was already midnight and Holkar was getting ready to take leave of his guest when Ali entered the courtyard and, without saying a word, moved towards his master, his hands held out in the shape of a cup.

'Who is there? What do you want?' asked Holkar.

'Can I speak to you, my Lord?' replied the servant, giving Corcoran a sidelong glance to indicate that he wanted to be alone with his master.

Corcoran was about to withdraw discreetly but Holkar held him back.

'Stay,' he said to Corcoran. 'And you,' turning to Ali, 'tell me quickly.'

He was a fakir, half-naked, the colour of bronze

'My Lord,' said Ali, 'a messenger has just come from Tantia Tope.'[18]

'From Tantia Tope!' exclaimed Holkar, whose eyes suddenly gleamed with joy. 'Send him in.'

The messenger entered the court. He was a fakir, half-naked, the colour of bronze, on whose impassive face one could detect neither pain nor pleasure.

He prostrated himself before Holkar, and waited in silence until Holkar ordered him to stand up.

'Who are you?' said Holkar.

'I am called Sugriva.'

'Are you a Brahmin?'

'I am a Brahmin. Tantia Tope sent me.'

'What proof do you have that he sent you?' asked Holkar.

'This,' said the fakir.

From the loincloth which served as his only garment, he pulled an oddly shaped handkerchief on which were written some Sanskrit words.

'Aha!' exclaimed Holkar, after looking carefully at the handkerchief, 'it is nearly time, then…'

'Yes,' said the fakir, 'it should all start today in Meerut.'[19]

'Captain,' said Holkar turning to his guest, 'you told me earlier that you don't like the English.'

'I don't exactly detest them,' said Corcoran, 'but I don't really care what happens to them either.'

'Excellent, Captain. Before long we will have some good news, and Colonel Barclay and his army should have been forced back by the end of the month.'

'Really?' said Corcoran, 'and it was this dark man who brought you this news?'

He went peacefully to bed

'Yes,' said Holkar, 'he was sent by my friend Tantia Tope.'

'And who is your friend Tantia Tope?'

'I will tell you tomorrow. Colonel Barclay won't get here for three days. So we still have two days of freedom. Tomorrow, if you wish, we will go on a rhinoceros hunt. The rhinoceros is the prince of wild beasts, and there are only about two hundred of them in all of India. I bid you goodnight, Captain.'

'And by the way,' said Corcoran, 'what have you done with Rao? Will he face judgement?'

'Rao?' said Holkar. 'He has already been judged. Before dinner, I gave the order for him to be impaled.'

'Gadzooks,' exclaimed Corcoran, 'you are in a hurry, Lord Holkar.'

'My friend,' said Holkar, 'my maxim is arrest immediately and impale immediately. Would you have me assemble a Court of Justice like the one in Calcutta? Before the prosecutor could speak, and the lawyer could respond and the judge deliberate, the English would have reached Bhagavpur, and they would have saved the life of this scoundrel – their accomplice, after all. No – he is responsible, and he shall pay.'

'Ah, I see,' said Corcoran, who had begun stretching his arms, for he longed to go to sleep. 'I only raised the matter out of curiosity. Goodnight, Lord Holkar.'

And Corcoran left, following Ali, who showed the way, and he went peacefully to bed.

6

A traitor escapes

But fate had already decided that the brave Captain would not sleep peacefully that night, for no sooner had he lain down on his bed than he heard a great noise. He sat up, and resting on one elbow, whistled gently at Louison and said to her in a low voice, 'Louison! Attention! Get up, lazybones.'

Louison looked at him; her ears pricked up, her tail wagging gently to acknowledge the Captain's words. She got up slowly and went straight to the door of the bedroom. She listened carefully, and returned silently towards Corcoran, as if she was now awaiting his orders.

'Good,' he said, 'I understand what you are telling me, my dear. You think that there is no pressing danger. Very good, because I would like to sleep a little. And you?'

The tigress parted her whiskered lips slightly – this was her way of smiling.

But before long footsteps could be heard in the corridor, and Louison returned to listen at the door. However, the danger still didn't seem very important to her, so she lay down again at her master's feet. Someone then knocked on the door.

Corcoran got up, half-dressed, revolver in hand and opened the door – Ali had come to wake them.

'My Lord,' he said, with a fearful look, 'Prince Holkar would like to see you. A great misfortune has occurred. Rao, who we thought had been impaled, in fact bribed his guards, and has fled with them.'

'Well,' said Corcoran, 'he's no idiot, this Rao!'

As they spoke, Corcoran finished getting dressed.

'And what is more, my Lord,' said Ali, 'His Highness believes that Rao will now join the English, who are already close by. Sugriva has seen them.'

'Well, show me the way.'

Holkar was sitting on a magnificent Persian carpet, and appeared to be absorbed in his thoughts. When the Captain entered, he raised his head and signalled that Corcoran should sit down beside him. Then he ordered his servants to leave.

'My dear guest,' he said, 'have you heard about my misfortune?'

'I've been told,' replied Corcoran. 'Rao has escaped – but that's not such a misfortune. He's a scoundrel who will be caught sooner or later.'

'Yes, but he took with him two hundred of my horsemen, and they've all gone to join the English.'

'Hmmm, hmmm,' muttered Corcoran pensively.

And seeing that Holkar appeared utterly downcast by this act of treason, he thought it necessary to restore his spirits and his courage.

'Ah well,' he said, with a smile on his face, 'that's two

hundred fewer traitors, after all. Good thing. Would you prefer that they were with you in Bhagavpur, ready to hand you over to Colonel Barclay?'

'And to think,' exclaimed Holkar, 'that just an hour earlier I had heard such good news.'

'About your Tantia Tope?'

'Yes. Now listen, Captain, after the service you have rendered me this evening, I can no longer have any secrets from you. You see, all of India is ready to take up arms.'

'For what purpose?'

'To get rid of the English.'

'Ah,' said Corcoran, 'now I understand. Get rid of the English! Well, Lord Holkar, if they were in my dear Brittany as they are here in India, I would pick them up one by one, by the collar and the waistband, and throw them into the sea to fatten the porpoises. Get rid of the English! I approve of that, Lord Holkar, and I'll even give you a helping hand. Good! I'll forget about my scientific duties, and Sir William Barrowlinson's letter... and that promise of mine not to get mixed up in politics so long as I am between the Himalayan mountains and Cape Comorin... And, it's a great idea – throwing out the English. Whose idea was it?'

'Everyone's,' replied Holkar. 'Tantia Tope's, Nana Sahib's,[20] mine, all the world's...'

'All the world?' exclaimed Corcoran, laughing. 'I'm sure. And you say you are going to throw them out?'

'That's our hope at least,' said Holkar, 'though I fear I may not live to see it happen. That Rao, my Prime Minister, has for the last three months been advising Colonel Barclay in the hope of obtaining, in return for his treason, my land and my daughter. I got wind of this, and beat him fifty times with a stick. That's how it all started…'

'What? That hideous creature hoped to become your son-in-law?' asked Corcoran indignantly.

'Yes,' said Holkar, 'that son of a dog, whose father was a Parsee merchant from Bombay, wanted to marry the daughter of the last of the Raghuvids, the most noble race in Asia.'[21]

It must be said that the Captain, who hadn't until then been especially interested in Holkar's story, began to be very attentive.

From then on, Corcoran's only desire was to catch Rao, and have him impaled. Rao had dared to aspire to the hand of Sita, the most beautiful woman in India! An angel of grace, of beauty, of innocence. The only way for Rao to escape impalement would be if he were hanged first from the gallows.

These were the reflections of the Captain. If you are astonished to see the sudden interest he was showing in a young woman of whom, a day earlier, he knew neither the name nor the face, I should tell you that he is a man of first instincts. A man who loves adventures (without being an adventurer), and who is certainly not displeased to be given the responsibility for protecting a young and beautiful princess in distress, especially one who is in distress because of the English.

'Lord Holkar,' he said, 'there is only one path to follow. Leave the rhinoceros hunt for another day, and pursue Rao until death. The scoundrel can't be far from here.'

'Alas,' said Holkar, 'I was thinking that too, but he had an eight-hour start on us, and he must have reached the English camp by now. So, let's make the best of it, without delay. I've already given my orders for the hunt. We'll leave at around six, when the sun rises, for after that the sun becomes unbearable. We'll leave my daughter behind, well-guarded, in case Rao has spies in the palace, and we should be back by ten o'clock. Ali will remain in the palace all that time, and Sugriva will get the latest news by scouting around the neighbourhood.'

'But,' said Corcoran, 'why should we go on a rhinoceros hunt today, if you fear some danger?'

'My dear guest,' replied Holkar, 'the last of the Raghuvids does not want to perish, if he must perish, hidden away in his palace like a bear in his cave. That's not the example set by my ancestor Rama, who defeated Ravana, the prince of demons.'

'Very well,' said Corcoran, who could not help feeling that something might go wrong, 'at least let me leave your daughter in the care of a bodyguard more trustworthy, more redoubtable than Ali and the entire Bhagavpur garrison.'

'And who is this friend who is so trustworthy and formidable?'

'Why Louison, of course!'

At that moment, the tigress, who could see that they were speaking about her, stood up on her hind legs and put her front paws on Corcoran's shoulders.

At this point Sita arrived.

'My dear child,' said Holkar, 'tomorrow we are going on a rhinoceros hunt.'

'With me?' interrupted the young woman.

'No, you must remain in the palace. That traitor Rao is wandering around the countryside with his horsemen, and I don't want you meeting him by chance.'

'But my father,' said Sita, who was clearly looking forward

to the hunt, 'I'm a good rider, as you know, and I wouldn't leave your side for an instant.'

'Perhaps she would be safer with us,' added Corcoran. 'I promise to watch over her, and if Rao comes close, I'll make sure he ends up in the jaws of Louison.'

'No,' said the old man, 'a chance meeting would be too dangerous, and I prefer to accept the offer you made on Louison's behalf.'

'Really, Monsieur?' said Sita, clapping her hands with joy, 'you'll give me Louison for the whole day?'

'You could have her forever,' replied the Breton, 'if I thought she would willingly be given away; but she is a bit capricious and she doesn't always listen to me. Now Louison, you won't be with me for a while, not until I get back. You must look after this beautiful princess. If someone tries to talk to her, you must growl; if someone displeases her, you can have him for your breakfast. If she wants to walk in the garden, you should accompany her, and you should regard her at all times as your mistress and sovereign. Are your duties clear to you?'

Louison looked back and forth between her master and Sita, and purred with pleasure.

'Good, you've understood,' continued Corcoran. 'Prove it now by lying down at the feet of the princess, and kissing her hand.'

Louison didn't hesitate. She lay down, and responded to Sita's caresses by licking her hands in a slightly ungracious manner.

'Such a guard,' said Corcoran, 'is worth a squadron of cavalry in terms of vigilance and courage, and as for intelligence, there is no equal. She will never commit an indiscretion. She doesn't like flattery. She knows how to distinguish real friends from those who want to trick her. And she's not too greedy. A little raw meat is fine for her. She is particularly talented as a judge of character, and she has more than a hundred times managed to sort out an embarrassing situation with just a single roar.'

'Lord Corcoran,' said Sita, 'such a friendship is more valuable than all the money in the world. And I'm delighted to accept Louison's friendship, and give mine in return.'

While they were talking, the sun had risen. Corcoran kissed Louison's forehead one last time, bowed respectfully to Sita and mounted his horse, as did Holkar – followed by a group of four or five hundred men. Louison watched them leave with regret, but finally she seemed to resign herself to their absence. Sita called to her, and Louison returned to the palace where, lying listlessly on the veranda she waited, like the Princess, for the return of the hunters.

7

The rhinoceros hunt

Unfortunately, Louison, in spite of all her fine qualities, was of the age when tigresses need their mothers. No sooner had she seen the group of hunters disappear over the horizon, and smelled the delicious perfume of the forests which the breeze carried in her direction, than she wanted to leave at triple gallop and catch up with Captain Corcoran, leaving behind the palace and her duties as a bodyguard, the importance of which she did not really understand.

Simply put, she was capricious, vain, frivolous and pleasure-loving. Perhaps she was also just dreaming about a rhinoceros hunt. But we will never know for sure, since it was never one of her defects to tell a stranger what she was thinking.

Whatever the truth, she yawned so loudly, stretched out on the ground in all directions with so much languor, and even took to roaring a little out of boredom that Sita, in spite of her wish to keep Louison with her, started to worry about her companion, and finally let her leave.

Hardly had the gate of the palace opened than the tigress

leapt through the air, clearing with one bound the hedgerow that separated the garden from the rest of the city, flying over the head of an astonished watchman. She then crossed two or three roads, knocking over without warning two or three dozen shopkeepers who were standing peacefully on the street, before arriving at the main gate of the city of Bhagavpur. The soldiers on guard refrained from stopping her, and conferred on her the same honour they would a senior officer, by hurrying back to their barracks and grabbing their rifles to fire in the air. Louison did not deign to respond.

As she ran through the countryside, she gathered important information, looking carefully for the route which the horses had taken, and with her nose high in the air, she was like a fine hunting dog searching for its prey.

Meanwhile, Prince Holkar and Captain Corcoran were in hunting mode, and whatever had been troubling them earlier, they talked with great gaiety and seemed to be thinking only of rhinoceroses.

'Have you hunted rhinoceros before?' Holkar asked the Breton.

'Never,' he responded. 'I've hunted tiger, elephant, hippopotamus, lion and panther, but the rhinoceros is an unknown animal for me. I've never even seen one, not even in a zoo.'

'It's a very rare and very precious animal,' said Holkar. 'It's pretty large when it is full-grown. I've seen two or three of them that were at least six feet high and twelve or fifteen feet long. The rhinoceros is heavy, massive; its skin is rough, and harder than armour. Its head is short, its ears are upright and alert like those of a horse. Its snout is stubby, and on top is a single horn which is its main weapon. You will see within the hour just how it uses that horn. If we are lucky in the hunt, which isn't certain, since its skin is bulletproof, and it is more robust than all other animals, including even the elephant, then I promise that we will have rhinoceros steak for dinner. And that's not something to sniff at. Rhinoceros steak, you know, is eaten only at the table of princes.'

As they were talking, Holkar and Corcoran reached what was known as the Crossroads of the Four Palm Trees at the entrance to the forest.

'Let's stop here,' said Holkar, getting down from his horse. 'Our horses cannot stand the sight or smell of a rhinoceros. We must ride elephants.'

A group of elephants was ready and harnessed in advance, waiting for the main hunters.

'What's the purpose of that man up front,' asked the Captain, 'the one who is practically sitting on the ears of the elephant?'

'He's the lead rider,' replied Holkar. 'Only he can get the animal to listen and obey.'

'And the other one?' continued the Captain, 'the one sitting respectfully behind me, who seems to be waiting for my orders?'

'My dear guest, he's the one who will be eaten.'

'Eaten by whom? I'm not hungry, and I don't imagine that's the kind of food you would order for me, would you?'

'Eaten by the tiger, Captain.'

'By the tiger! What tiger? We're hunting rhinoceros, I thought, not tigers.'

'My dear friend,' said Holkar, laughing, 'that's just an English custom that we have adopted. And it's an excellent one as you shall see. The English noticed that one often meets in our forests an animal which one didn't expect – a tiger, for example, or a jaguar or a panther. Now, all these animals that get up early in the morning like us, that get hungry like us, and that live by hunting, and that have no other means of existence – well they often wait for a traveller on the corner of a path, in the hope of breakfast. Moreover, since they don't like to attack a human whose face they can see, they almost always jump on you from behind, at the moment you least expect it, and carry you off into the jungle to eat at their leisure.

'Now the English are very sensitive, very prudent – true gentlemen, who regard their skin as more precious in the eyes of the Eternal Being than those of all other human beings. And the English, I tell you, invented the notion of placing upon the elephant, when they go for a walk or out hunting, apart from the elephant handler, a poor devil who serves as the tiger's prey. If by chance some misfortune should occur, it would not be right if a gentleman were exposed to the possibility of being eaten rather than the poor devil. And, after all, Divine Providence has created poor devils so that they can be eaten in the place of gentlemen.

'Isn't this an admirable reason, my dear friend? And aren't you now at ease in knowing that the boy who is at the back will become a steak for the tiger rather than you?'

'Certainly not!' said Corcoran, 'let us dismount immediately and return to Bhagavpur, by the shortest possible route. If I had to serve as fodder or bait to anyone, man or beast, I hope I would at least have the chance to defend myself and... But what is the meaning of this?'

The elephants had all raised their trunks as a sign of great fear. And the elephant handlers realised that they were no longer in control of their animals.

'It means,' replied Holkar, 'that there is something here in the jungle that we cannot see and which, to judge by the terror of the elephants, is very dangerous. Be on guard, Captain, and keep looking around you.'

At that same moment, many of the horses reared up, and several riders were thrown to the ground, and the elephants began to take flight, in spite of their handlers' efforts.

It was Louison who was causing all this commotion. She arrived at a great gallop, leaping over ditches, hedges and bushes, as fast as a train at top speed.

Seeing her, everyone reached for their weapons, but Corcoran reassured them.

'You have nothing to fear,' he said, 'it's my dear Louison... And you, Mademoiselle,' he continued, looking at her as if he wanted to be severe, 'what are you doing here?'

Louison didn't reply, but wagged her tale in a deliberate manner as if she was trying to tell the Captain something.

'Oh, I see. You were bored at the palace. Mademoiselle wanted to hunt a rhinoceros. Is that right? Louison, I don't like it that you are so untroubled when you have done something bad. Well? Yes, I can read your eyes. Anyway, come with me, follow the hunt, be sensible and try not to scare anyone.'

Delighted by her favourable reception and by the Captain's permission to join the hunt, Louison was soon forgiven for her sudden arrival. She became, in just a short time, the best of friends with all of Holkar's escort, men and beasts, or at least no one dared to tell her how much pleasure they would have had if she had been locked up in a good strong cage, fifteen hundred leagues away from Bhagavpur.

Before long, Holkar's trackers declared that they were on the trail of the rhinoceros, which would soon emerge on a path where several of the hunters had gathered, including Holkar and Captain Corcoran.

And it wasn't long before the animal appeared, followed by the trackers who threw stones at him, without doing him any harm. These stones, big as they were, bounced off his thick body armour like balls of bread off a rifleman's helmet. He trotted on without showing any emotion or any sense that he might be intimidated by such a large number of adversaries.

'Pay attention everybody and prepare yourselves,' said Holkar. 'Here he is. The only places where you can harm him are his eyes or his ears, and you can only fire at him from the side, because from the front his body is so well protected.'

Holkar had hardly finished speaking when everyone opened fire. More than sixty bullets hit the animal at the same time, but not one of them could pierce his skin. Only Corcoran had held fire, and it was fortunate that he did so.

The rhinoceros, either shaken or irritated by this attack, lifted his head, and began to run in their direction at great speed and with quite terrifying determination. He butted Corcoran's elephant with his horn.

After this unexpected attack, the injured elephant tottered and then tried to seize its enemy with its trunk and smash it against a tree or a rock. But the rhinoceros didn't allow himself to be caught, and instead mounted a second attack with his horn, and he drove it into the heart of the elephant, which fell heavily to the ground, like a great oak that had been uprooted.

The rhinoceros pulled away from the dying elephant, and headed straight for Corcoran, who was about to be knocked to the ground like his unfortunate mount.

The Captain was in a terrifying situation. Even the bravest of the other hunters dared not come close, and Corcoran himself had a foot trapped in the elephant's harness and was unable even to stand up.

'Come here, Louison!' he shouted.

Fortunately, the tigress had not waited to be asked. She had been following the hunt as a spectator, as if she were only there to witness the action. But as soon as she saw that her friend was in danger, she leapt forward, spinning around the rhinoceros, and grabbed the animal by the ears in such a way that he couldn't move.

Thanks to Louison's speedy arrival Corcoran was able to release himself and was standing upright beside his enemy.

'Bravo, my Louison,' he said. 'Hold it tight. Yes, like that. Wait, I will find the most vulnerable spot. Ah, that's it.'

And he placed the muzzle of his gun in the ear of the rhinoceros and fired. The animal, mortally injured, suffered a final massive convulsion, which threw Louison some fifteen paces on to the shoulders of one of the hunters, and the rhinoceros fell to the ground stone-dead.

'My dear guest,' said Holkar, 'you are blessed by good fortune. I would give half my kingdom to have a friend as tenacious, as faithful, as brave and as skilful as Louison. For today the hunt is over. Tomorrow we will perhaps find something even better... Let's go.'

They lifted the rhinoceros and put it on a cart, and set off on the road to Bhagavpur.

On the journey back, Louison received repeated words of gratitude from her master, and she responded with many leaps of joy at having been able to save him.

However, the return was not as cheerful as might have been anticipated. Each of them seemed to have a premonition of some great misfortune. Corcoran, without saying so, reproached himself for having agreed to the hunt. Holkar reproached himself still more for having proposed it, and both of them feared for Sita.

Suddenly, about half a league from Bhagavpur, from the top of a hill where one could see the Narmada Valley and the city, they spotted thick smoke rising from the suburbs, and they could hear confusing sounds, distant and thudding, dominated by the thunder of artillery, the firing of rifles and the screams of women and children.

'Lord Holkar,' said Corcoran, 'do you hear what I hear, and see what I see? Bhagavpur is on fire or has been attacked.'

Holkar turned pale.

'And my daughter,' he exclaimed, 'my poor Sita.'

Holkar dug his spurs into the belly of his horse and left at a great gallop. Corcoran followed him at the same pace. The rest of the escort, even though they were moving at speed, remained a long way behind.

Holkar and Corcoran arrived at the nearest gate and began questioning one of the officers.

'My Lord,' he said to Holkar, 'I don't know what happened. The fire started in five or six places at once, and even inside Your Highness's palace, but…'

He was going to continue, but Holkar was no longer listening to him.

'Inside my palace!' he exclaimed, and digging in his spurs, he galloped off in a greater fury than ever. Without saying a word, Corcoran followed, with Louison running beside them.

Everything was in disarray in the palace. There were large pools of blood on the main staircase. There were bodies lying in the corridors. Almost all of Holkar's servants were dead.

On seeing this the old man began pulling his hair out.

'Alas!' he said, 'where is Sita?'

Suddenly Ali appeared. He'd been stabbed in the chest with a dagger, but the wound was not mortal.

'Ali! Ali! What have you done with my daughter?' asked Holkar in a voice that resounded through the palace.

'My Lord,' exclaimed Ali throwing himself on the ground, 'forgive me. They have taken her.'

'My daughter has been taken!' said Holkar, 'and you, dog-face, you did nothing to save her. Where is she? Who took her? Speak! Speak now!'

'My Lord,' said Ali, 'it was Rao. He had spies in the palace. The Princess was ambushed by men who stabbed most of your servants to death, and who carried her away by boat in spite of her screams and tears. They took her to the other bank of the river, where Rao was waiting with his horsemen, and they all left together. It's not known in which direction, but they took the precaution of mooring all the other boats on the far bank of the river so that they couldn't be followed.'

Holkar, overwhelmed by misfortune, heard nothing. But Corcoran, also shaken by this unexpected event, could only think about how to save Sita.

'So where did all the smoke come from that we saw rising above the city?' Corcoran asked.

There were bodies lying in the corridors

'Alas, Lord Corcoran,' replied Ali, 'the bandits, to ensure that they were successful, set fire to five or six areas of the city. But the fires were quickly put out.'

'Well,' said Corcoran, 'it will be necessary to swim across to the boats on the other side, and then we can start off in pursuit of the kidnappers.'

'Captain, it's even worse than you think,' said Ali. 'We've just learnt that the vanguard of the English army is only five leagues from here, and that was what probably gave the miserable Rao the audacity to come and face us in Bhagavpur. Already, one of their cavalry detachments has been spotted nearby.'

'And what if they come now?' exclaimed the desperate Holkar. 'What if they take my city, my money and my life? I've lost my darling daughter, who is alone worth the price of all that. I've lost everything.'

Corcoran took his hand and spoke firmly.

'Be a man, my host,' he said, 'and take courage. Your daughter has been kidnapped, but she is not dead, nor has she been dishonoured. We will find her, I promise you that... Oh, why didn't Louison stay with her? She wouldn't have been stabbed, or terrified or bribed like your unfortunate servants. But what happened has happened. Holkar, I'm leaving now.'

'You're leaving me! At such a time?'

'My dear host, I forgive you such an unjust suspicion. I'm going to chase after that miserable Rao, catch him, and hang him myself from the nearest tree.'

'Yes, that's the right thing to do.' Holkar was suddenly revived by the thought of finding his daughter. 'And I will come with you.'

'No! Stay here!' said Corcoran. 'Stay here to lead the

investigation, and to stand up to the English who will besiege your city. For me, there is nothing to keep me here. I will find Sita, and bring her back to you, I hope. Come on, Louison, my dear, it's your fault we lost her, so it's up to you to bring her back… Go and find her…'

He took Sita's scarf, still perfumed with the scent of irises, and waved it in front of Louison's nose.

'That's her. That's Sita whom we must bring back,' said Corcoran. 'Find her!'

Meanwhile, Holkar's boatmen, who had swum across the river, managed to bring back the boat in which Sita had been taken away. Immediately, Louison and her master went on board, along with a horse and two boatmen.

Corcoran, after crossing the Narmada, set foot on the other side with Louison, and once again he waved Sita's scarf in front of her nose. Louison immediately understood what was expected of her and she headed off down a little-used path which ended in a large clearing, where it was easy, from the trampled ground, to work out that a troop of cavalry had recently passed by.

From there, she took a larger, well-maintained road. Corcoran followed her on horseback at a fast trot.

One league further on, Louison spotted a piece of Sita's dress which must have caught on a bush, and with a suggestive glance brought it to the attention of the Captain. He jumped down from his horse, picked up the precious piece of cloth, placed it next to his heart, and they continued on their way.

He soon heard the sound of the troop of cavalry coming from one side – and he had high hopes of immediately finding Sita and her kidnappers. But he was mistaken. It was a squadron of the 25th Regiment of the English cavalry.

Corcoran gestured to Louison to stay where she was, and he moved forward to meet the newcomers.

'Who goes there?' shouted the officer in a powerful voice.

'A friend!' replied Corcoran.

'Who are you?' asked the English officer.

The officer was a large young man with red hair, sideburns and broad shoulders. One would imagine him to be an excellent horseman, a powerful boxer, and a fine player of cricket.

'I am a Frenchman,' said Corcoran.

'What are you doing here?' asked the officer.

The imperious and brusque tone of the Englishman did not please the Breton, who responded dryly.

'I'm going for a walk.'

'Monsieur,' said the Englishman, 'I'm not in the mood for jokes. We're in enemy country, and I have the right to know who you are.'

'That's very true,' replied Corcoran. 'Well, I come here in search of the famous manuscript of the laws of Manu, the *Guru Karamta*,[22] which I have been told is hidden inside an unknown temple. You wouldn't know where it is, would you?'

The Englishman looked at him suspiciously, not knowing whether Corcoran was speaking seriously or was mocking him.

'You have, I imagine, some documents that can prove your identity?' he asked.

'Do you recognize this seal?'

'No.'

'Well, it's the seal of Sir William Barrowlinson, director of the East India Company and the President of the Geographical, Colonial, Orographical and Photographical Society, and doubtless you will know of him.'

'Do I know him! It was he who got me my commission as a lieutenant in the Indian army.'

'Ah, good,' continued Corcoran, 'here is a letter of recommendation provided to me by that gentleman.'

'That baronet, if you please!' interrupted the officer.

'That baronet, if that title pleases you, gave it to me to show to the Governor-General in Calcutta.'

'Very good,' said the officer. 'And where have you just come from?'

'From Bhagavpur.'

'Ah you have seen that rebel, Holkar. So, is he ready to surrender? Or is he preparing to fight?'

'Monsieur,' said Corcoran, 'you'll be able to judge for yourself when you get closer to Bhagavpur.'

'But tell me at least whether he has a large well-disciplined army.'

'I know nothing of such things… And now, Messieurs, would you kindly let me continue on my way?'

'Patience, Monsieur,' said the officer, 'who is to say you are not Holkar's spy?'

Corcoran gave the Englishman a cold, fixed stare.

'Monsieur,' he said, 'if you were alone in the open countryside with me, perhaps you would be more polite.'

'Monsieur,' said the Englishman in turn, 'I don't worry about whether I am polite or not, I just do my duty. Follow us to our headquarters.'

'I would be most obliged if you would show me the way,' said the Breton.

He had made up his mind that the best means of discovering where Sita had been taken was to go to the headquarters of the

English army, where he was certain Rao would have sought sanctuary.

'But,' he added, 'would you permit me to bring along a friend?'

'Certainly, Monsieur,' said the Englishman, 'you can bring as many friends as you please.'

Corcoran whistled, and suddenly Louison appeared. From seeing Corcoran, to moving towards him, and then being at his side all took just an instant. The cavalry horses were seized by a great terror, and tried to unseat their riders and run away across the plains.

As for the riders, they were just as perturbed as their horses, but it was a matter of military honour that they controlled themselves, and did not take flight.

'Monsieur,' said the officer, 'that's a pretty strong joke. Where did you find this friend of yours?'

'I'm surprised by your surprise,' replied the Breton. 'You lot, you English, you play all kinds of sport; you chase after horses, dogs, foxes, cockerels and all the beasts of creation… As for me, I prefer tigers. Each to his own taste. You wouldn't be scared by such a companion, by any chance?'

'Monsieur,' said the Englishman angrily, 'an English gentleman fears nothing. But I do ask myself if a tiger is really a suitable companion for a gentleman.'

'Louison is perhaps asking herself the same question at this moment,' said Corcoran in turn, 'and wondering if the company of an Englishman is really suitable for her. Anyway, we should introduce ourselves. Lieutenant, what is your name?'

'John Robarts, Monsieur,' replied the Englishman in a manner that was both stiff and arrogant.

'Very good,' continued Corcoran. 'Now pay attention, Louison. I present to you the very honourable John Robarts, Lieutenant of the Queen's 25th Hussars… Now listen, you must take care to use neither your teeth nor your claws against him, except in the case of legitimate defence.'

'Monsieur,' said the Englishman, 'surely you will bring to an end this unseemly comedy.'

'And to you, Lieutenant John Robarts,' said Corcoran without emotion, 'I have the honour of presenting Miss Louison, my best friend… Now, Lieutenant, you may think I lack respect for your uniform, but I am an honourable man, and ready to explain myself.'

'That's good, Monsieur,' said Robarts, 'we will see about all that later… We're leaving now. Follow us.'

The journey did not take long.

The English camp was just a quarter of a league away, beside a stream which flowed into the Narmada. The horses, the soldiers, the cooks and all the trappings which accompany an army in India were grouped together in picturesque disorder.

John Robarts, accompanied by Corcoran and Louison, entered Colonel Barclay's tent.

8

An emotional conversation between Louison, Captain Corcoran and Colonel Barclay

Colonel Barclay, now an acting Brigadier-General, was one of the most courageous officers in the English army in India. He had risen painstakingly through the ranks, and was always, in peacetime and during war, given the most difficult missions. Whether he was the commander of a frontier regiment, or a Resident in a princely state overseeing diplomatic manoeuvres against its ruler, he had both the confidence of his fellow soldiers and a deep understanding of English policy towards India. Because he had no brother, or uncle, or son or nephew among the directors of the East India Company, he was given only the most undesirable or perilous missions.

It's for this reason that he was chosen for the attack on Holkar.

If he succeeded, then his well-connected general would be in a good position to become army commander, as a reward for Barclay's victory. And because of this Colonel Barclay was always in a bad mood. He resented, understandably, the favourites of the most-exalted and most-powerful East India Company, though this bad mood never prevented him from carrying out his military duties most rigorously.

When John Robarts entered his tent, Barclay turned and said, 'So what news do you have, Robarts?'

'We have made an important arrest, Colonel. A Frenchman who is, I think, Holkar's spy.'

'That's good. Send him in.'

'But,' said Robarts, 'he is not alone.'

'Fine. Send in the others too, and put two guards at the entrance of the tent.'

'But Colonel…'

'Do what I said, and don't answer back.'

'Well then,' thought Robarts, 'if he doesn't want to listen to what I have to say that's his problem.'

Robarts gestured to Corcoran.

'Go in,' he said.

Corcoran entered, preceded by Louison, who – at the Captain's signal – lay down at his feet. She was hidden from view by the table which separated Corcoran from Colonel Barclay.

Barclay, his back turned, pretended not to have noticed or heard Corcoran. And because of this, he hadn't noticed the presence of Louison.

There were a few moments of silence. Corcoran, seeing that the Colonel hadn't spoken to him, and hadn't asked him to sit, sat down anyway, picked up a book from the table, and pretended to read it with great interest.

Eventually, Barclay realized that the prisoner was not the type who was easily intimidated, and turned towards him.

'Who are you?' he asked abruptly.

'A Frenchman.'

'Your name?'

'Corcoran.'

'Your profession?'

'Sailor and scholar.'

'Why do you call yourself a scholar?'

'I am searching for the manuscript of the *Guru Karamta* on behalf of the Academy of Sciences of Lyon.'

'And where were you going when you ran into us?'

'I was searching for a young woman who has been kidnapped from her father by a brigand.'

'Is she Indian or English?'

'She's the daughter of Holkar, Prince of the Marathas.'

Colonel Barclay examined Corcoran with a challenging look.

'What interest do you take in the affairs of Holkar?' he asked.

'I am his guest,' Corcoran replied firmly.

'Really!' said Barclay. 'Do you have any letters of recommendation?'

Corcoran gave him the letter from Sir William Barrowlinson.

'That's good,' said Barclay, after reading the letter. 'I see that you are a gentleman. You can reassure Holkar about the fate of his daughter. She is in my camp. Rao brought her here barely two hours ago. She's a precious hostage for us, but no harm has or will come to her. The honour of the English army depends on it, and Rao himself respects that, even if he wishes to marry her, as the prize of his victory…'

'Or rather his infamous treason.'

'As you please, the words mean little to me… And now, Monsieur Corcoran, if you would like to see the beautiful Sita for yourself, and tell her father that she is safe and sound, and in trustworthy hands, you can. I'll call for her.'

'I hadn't even ventured to ask you for that, Colonel – so I would like to thank you for having made the offer.'

The Colonel banged on a gong, and John Robarts appeared immediately. He had been waiting with impatience and curiosity for the end of the meeting. He was very surprised to see Corcoran sitting comfortably at the table, opposite the Colonel, and Louison between the two of them, hidden from the Colonel by the tablecloth.

'Robarts,' said Barclay, 'go and find Miss Sita, and bring her here with all the respect that an English gentleman owes to a woman of the highest rank.'

'But Colonel…' replied Robarts, who wanted to warn Barclay of the presence of Louison.

'I see you still haven't left, Sir,' said Barclay with haughty disdain.

Robarts, forced to obey, left with his head down.

'You don't know the Narmada Valley, I suppose, Monsieur?' asked Barclay in the tone of a tourist who is praising the beauty of the countryside. 'It's an enchanting land. One can find places that are one thousand times as beautiful as the Alps or the Pyrenees. Believe me, Monsieur, I've lived here for nine years, without any company but the stones of the mountains, and of spies who report everything that I do to Holkar. Ah, Monsieur, what a boring job it is to receive, analyse, classify and evaluate police reports… Are you interested in geology? No. Never mind. Geology is my passion. If only you were keen on geology what an excellent eight days we could have spent together, because it won't take longer than eight days to overthrow Holkar. Maybe you wouldn't like that, because of your friendship with him. That's fine, let's speak no more of that. I hope, Monsieur, you will do me the honour of dining with me tonight.'

Corcoran said that he would not be able to accept his invitation.

'I understand! You fear that the dinner won't be very good. I can see why… But be reassured. We have excellent French wine and pâtés from France, and puddings from England, and every exquisite delicacy that the world produces for the pleasure of gentlemen. So there we are.'

'Colonel,' said Corcoran, 'I regret that I cannot accept such a cordial offer, but I am in a hurry to reassure Holkar about his daughter.'

'Reassure Holkar? My dear Sir! Don't even think of it. I am holding you here, and I will keep you here. You can write to Holkar. That should be enough. Do you think I would let you return to the enemy camp after you have seen mine? I will set you free when we have taken Bhagavpur.'

'And if you never take it, Colonel?' asked Corcoran who was becoming indignant at being treated like a prisoner of war.

'Well, if we never take it,' replied the Colonel, 'then you will never return there. That's what I'm telling you. And the Academy of Sciences of Lyon and all the academies under the sun will miss out on reading the manuscript of the *Guru Karamta*.'

'Colonel,' said Corcoran, 'you are breaking the law of nations.'

'I beg your pardon?'

At that moment, Sita appeared, and her presence suddenly eased the tension between the two men, who became more animated.

'Ah,' Sita exclaimed on seeing Corcoran, her eyes full of joy, 'I knew you would come and find me here.'

On hearing these words, an immense feeling of pleasure filled the heart of Captain Corcoran. She had been counting on him! She was waiting for him to save her!

But this wasn't the right time to reveal how he felt. Corcoran feared that at any moment Robarts or someone else might enter and foil the escape plan he was drawing up.

'So Colonel,' he said, 'do you refuse to set me free?'

'I refuse,' said Barclay

'So are you going to continue, against all the rules of natural justice, to hold Princess Sita, kidnapped from her father by a scoundrel who wants to become her husband?'

'You seem to think you can interrogate me,' said Barclay haughtily. He put out his hand and prepared to strike the gong.

'Ah well,' exclaimed Corcoran getting up, 'we will have to see what the heavens decide.'

And before Barclay could call anyone, Corcoran seized the gong, and put it out of reach. He then pulled a revolver from his pocket, and poked its muzzle into the Colonel's cheek.

'If you shout, I will blow your brains out.'

Barclay crossed his arms with a look of defiance.

'So I am dealing with an assassin, am I?' he said.

'No,' replied Corcoran, 'because you know that if you shout out, I will be killed. Then it is me who will be assassinated and you who will be the assassin. Those two roles are equally disagreeable. Let's make an agreement, if you are willing...'

'An agreement!' said Barclay. 'You expect me to make an agreement with a man I received as a gentleman, almost as a friend, and who pays me back by threatening to assassinate me.'

'That word again, Colonel!' said Corcoran. 'So we won't make an agreement, then, and I don't really need one. Stand up, Louison!'

With these words, the tigress got up, and showed herself for the first time to the astonished Barclay. The astonishment soon turned to fear.

'Louison,' continued Corcoran, 'take a close look at the Colonel. If he puts one foot outside the tent before the Princess and I are on horseback, he's all yours.'

Corcoran's threat was deadly serious, and Barclay knew it. He decided to give in.

'So what do you want?' he asked.

'I want you,' said Corcoran, 'to send for your two best horses. We will leave on horseback, the Princess and I. When we are beyond the boundaries of your camp, I will whistle. At that signal, the tigress will join me, and you will be free to send your cavalry after us, including Lieutenant John Robarts of the 25th Hussars, with whom I have a small account to settle. Is that agreed?'

'That's agreed,' said Barclay.

'And don't think you can break your sworn oath without paying for it,' added Corcoran, 'because Louison, who is more

The tigress got up and showed herself to the astonished Barclay

intelligent than many Christians, will know immediately and will grab you by the neck in an instant.'

'Monsieur,' said Barclay grandly, 'you can rely on the word of honour of an English gentleman.'

And so, without leaving the tent, he ordered Robarts to have two fine horses saddled and bridled. He watched Corcoran and Sita mount the horses, and greeted their goodbye waves with an air of indifference. He waited patiently until he heard the sound of a whistle.

As soon as Louison had begun to head in the same direction as Corcoran, taking great leaps through the air and terrifying everyone in the camp, Barclay shouted out:

'Ten thousand pounds sterling for whoever brings me that man and that woman alive!'

With these words, the camp filled with noisy discussion. All the horsemen hurriedly prepared their mounts, without even bothering to saddle them, so as not to lose time. As for the foot soldiers, they had already begun to run after the fugitives, and seemed to be moving as if they had wings.

Only Lieutenant Robarts, as he bridled his horse like the others, dared to question what had happened.

'Why did Colonel Barclay let them escape, if he is willing to spend so much on their recapture?'

To which the Colonel responded by having the speaker placed in detention for a month.

That's how it is. When the chief does something stupid, his subordinates must be silent. It is always dangerous to have more sense than one's chief.

9

At the gallop! At the gallop! Hurrah!

By now half the English cavalry was in pursuit of Corcoran and the beautiful Sita who were, in turn, galloping towards Bhagavpur, with the intrepid Louison at their side.

All three were well on their way, the first two on Colonel Barclay's best horses and Louison on her four paws, as they passed through plains, hills and valleys at the speed of an express train.[23] They were beginning to hope they had escaped their enemies when a great obstacle, unforeseen and almost insurmountable, appeared before them.

Corcoran saw a group of five or six horsemen dressed in red ahead of him.

They were English officers who had gone hunting, and who were slowly returning to the camp, followed by about thirty Indian servants, and several carts full of wild game and provisions.

On seeing them, Corcoran and Sita stopped, while Louison

sat gravely on her hind paws, ready to give them both her opinion as they met in council.

The Captain wouldn't have hesitated if he had been alone. He would have fearlessly tempted fate by riding straight through this little troop of Englishmen with Louison, but he feared risking, in such a dicey situation, the life or liberty of Sita.

Perhaps Corcoran was thinking it would have been better if he'd been doing what he'd been asked to do, namely searching for the manuscript of the *Guru Karamta*, rather than putting himself at the service of poor Holkar, whose cause seemed altogether desperate. But he immediately rejected this idea as unworthy of him.

Meanwhile, Sita was regarding him with great anxiety.

'So Captain, what are we going to do?' she asked.

'Have you made your decision?' replied the Captain.

'I will follow you,' said Sita.

'It's a question, you know, of getting through either by force or by trickery. I think we should try trickery, but if the English aren't fooled, it will be necessary to kill three or four of them, or die ourselves. Are you ready? Does none of this frighten you?'

'Captain,' said Sita, lifting her eyes to heaven, 'I only fear not seeing my father again, and of falling into the hands of the infamous Rao.'

'Good,' said the Breton. 'We'll be safe. Trot slowly on your horse. Behave normally. That will give us some time to breathe, but be ready. When I say "Brahma and Vishnu", you must gallop as fast as you can. Louison and I will be behind you.'

The three fugitives were in a fairly large valley, watered by the Hanuveri, a deep tributary of the Narmada. The two slopes of the valley were covered by tall palm trees and jungle in which all the great animals of India might be found – including tigers. And so it would not be wise to leave the main road and go down one of the few footpaths because you might suddenly be nose-to-nose with the most dreaded of all carnivores, not to speak of the terrifying snakes whose poison can strike one down more quickly than prussic acid.

Meanwhile, the English officers were moving towards them at a slow trot, with an air of nonchalance, as if they had no enemies to fear or to pursue. They had dined well, they were smoking Havana cigars, and discussing in a relaxed fashion some articles they had read in *The Times*.

They didn't seem to care about Corcoran, who had the dress and the unflappable appearance of a civilian – that's to say a civilian employed by the East India Company – though they were dazzled by the unusual beauty of Sita.

As for Louison, they were at first astonished, but since they were both Englishmen and sportsmen they well understood this sort of eccentricity, and one of them even attempted to buy the tigress.

'Are you coming from the camp, Sir?' he asked Corcoran.

'Yes,' replied the Breton.

'Good, do you have any news from England? The London mail must have arrived at midday.'

'Indeed, it has arrived.'

'So what's the latest West End gossip?' continued the Englishman. 'Is Lady Susan Carpeth still the most eligible young woman of Belgrave Square, or has Lady Margaret Cranmouth replaced her?'

'To tell you the truth,' replied the Breton, who didn't want, for fear of arousing suspicions, to show that he cared little for

Lady Susan or Lady Margaret, 'I fear that soon Miss Belinda Charters will overtake both these ladies.'

'Oh, really!' said the astonished gentleman. 'Miss Belinda Charters. Who is this new beauty, of whom I have never heard?'

'Well,' said Corcoran, 'that's no surprise. Mr William Charters is a gentleman who traded in wool and gold-dust in Australia and made a fortune of 75 or 80 million, and who...'

'75 or 80 million!' exclaimed the talkative and curious Englishman. 'That's a pretty sum.'

'Yes,' said Corcoran, 'and as you can imagine Miss Belinda Charters, who is also a great beauty, does not lack for suitors... We really must go now. Goodbye.'

And as he began to move off with Sita and Louison, the gentleman called him back.

'Sir, please excuse my indiscretion, but you should be warned that you are in enemy territory, and it could be dangerous to go down that route.'

'Thank you for your advice, Sir.'

'Holkar's scouts are fighting in this area, and you could be kidnapped by them.'

'Ah, really? Well, I will be careful.'

And Corcoran was about to continue on his way, but the Englishman, who seemed to have decided not to let him leave until sunset, tried once again to delay him.

'You are, I presume, an employee of the East India Company?'

'No, Sir, I travel for pleasure.'

The English gentleman nodded respectfully from his saddle, persuaded that a man who comes from Europe to India for his own pleasure must be a great nobleman, or at least a Lord or an influential member of the House of Commons.

He was about to open his mouth again, when Corcoran interrupted him. He heard behind him the sound of the horsemen who were following, and who would catch up with him soon.

'Excuse me, but I am in rather a hurry.'

'At least,' said the Englishman, 'let me offer you a cigar.'

'I do not smoke in the presence of women,' Corcoran replied impatiently.

The conversation until then had been in English, and the Breton could speak that language fluently. Unfortunately, the boredom of being stopped by a chatterbox, and of losing precious time, made him forget who he was talking to, and he said those last few words about not smoking in front of women in French.

'What the devil!' exclaimed the officer. 'You are a Frenchman, Monsieur, and not English. What are you doing here, on this road, at this time?'

The decisive moment was about to come. Corcoran glanced at Sita as a way of warning her to be ready to take flight.

She, meanwhile, had her eyes fixed on one of the Indians who were behind the English soldiers, and were driving their wagons. Corcoran realised to his astonishment that the Indian man and the daughter of Holkar were exchanging looks, without saying a word.

And then, looking more closely at the Indian, he recognised Sugriva, the Brahmin whom Tantia Tope had sent to Holkar.

Corcoran had little time to think, because ten English officers had surrounded him, and the one with whom he had been talking said, 'Monsieur, while we wait for an explanation of your presence in Holkar's territory, you are our prisoner.'

'Prisoner!' said Corcoran. 'You are joking. Move aside or I will kill you!'

He pulled his revolver from his pocket and took aim.

But just as quickly, the Englishman took aim with his revolver – and the two of them were ready to fire at each other, at point-blank range, until an unexpected incident settled the issue.

On hearing the sound of the two revolvers being cocked, Louison realised that there was about to be a battle. She leapt quickly on to the hindquarters of the Englishman's horse, which reared up and unsaddled its rider. That was fortunate for him and for our friend Corcoran, because the two adversaries were so close to each other that both their brains would have been blown out together, like the corks of two bottles of champagne.

The Englishman did manage to fire his pistol, but the bullet – diverted from its original target by Louison's great leap – removed the hat of another gentleman who had moved forward to seize Corcoran.

'Brahma and Vishnu!' shouted Corcoran.

On hearing the signal, Sita dug her spurs in, and her horse sped off like an arrow. Corcoran followed her, roughly pushing aside an Englishman who was trying to hold on to him. And Louison, seeing her two friends in flight, followed. The English barely had time to fire five or six pistol shots at them – one of which injured Corcoran's horse.

As for the Indian sepoys[24] who were driving the English wagons, and who were armed like their masters, not one of them moved, neither to help Corcoran nor to take him prisoner.

Alone among them, the Brahmin Sugriva, whom the others seemed to obey, performed a peculiar manoeuvre with his wagon, which led to a delay of three or four minutes in the English pursuit. He pretended that he wanted to turn round the wagon which was at the head of the column, and as a result of his eagerness, it overturned in the middle of the road.

Immediately the other Indians, as if obeying a command, left their wagons and gathered round the one that had overturned, blocking the road, entangling the carriages and horses, and forcing the English to stop in front of this living wall of men and animals.

At that moment, the horsemen from the camp, who were pursuing the fugitives, arrived on the scene. At the front galloped John Robarts,[25] who was seething with anger.

'Have you seen the Captain?' demanded Robarts.

'Which Captain?'

'That cursed, confounded Corcoran! Barclay is in a terrible fury. He let himself be played like a child, but won't admit it, and he has promised ten thousand pounds sterling to whoever brings him Captain Corcoran and Holkar's daughter.'

'What?' exclaimed one of the gentlemen. 'That was Holkar's daughter and we didn't realise it! I took her for, half-hidden behind her veil, a young English miss who was travelling through India with her future husband.'

'Let's go! Let's go!' said Robarts impatiently. 'A thousand guineas to whoever gets there first.'

At these words, a magical eagerness took hold of their hearts. With many cracks of the whip, they forced the Indians to move the wagons to the side of the road, and they headed off at triple gallop in pursuit of the fugitives.

The sun was setting quickly, as it does in the tropics, and the pursuit was all the more determined because there was so little daylight left.

10

Charge! Charge!

For his part, Corcoran was not going to be caught napping. He galloped alongside Sita, cursing the foolish curiosity of the English which had made him lose so much precious time.

However, he hoped that the approach of nightfall, the distance from the English camp, and some good luck, perhaps even the arrival of Holkar's vanguard, would give him time to reach Bhagavpur. But what made him angriest was being forced to flee.

'Flee from the English!' he thought. 'The shame of it! What would my father say if he saw me? My poor father, who never met an Englishman without suggesting they have a boxing match, or perhaps even kickboxing, or some other such game that gentlemen enjoy. And here I am, galloping away from them, right now, instead of picking up that cursed chatterbox by his cravat and throwing him in a ditch, as I wanted to do, and as it was my duty to do. My only thought was to make him believe that I was a *goddam*[26] like him. It felt as if I was banging my head against a wall.'

While having these thoughts, he realised suddenly that his horse was getting weaker, and his gallop, even though he dug his spurs in, was slowing to a trot. He looked down and saw that one of his boots was covered in blood. His horse had been hit in the side by a bullet.

But this new misfortune did not discourage the Breton.

He quickly dismounted.

'What are you doing?' asked Sita. 'Is this a moment to stop? The English are on our tail.'

'It's nothing, really,' said Corcoran, 'my horse was hit by a bullet when those cowardly scoundrels fired on us just now... Sita, if you want to flee, you'll have to go without me, but Louison will accompany you and defend you...'

'Yes,' said Sita, 'but who will defend me from Louison?'

Corcoran seemed concerned by this question.

'That's true,' he said. 'Louison has not had her dinner, and it's already late. I have no fears at all for you, but I'm not sure about your horse, or perhaps Louison will wander off searching for food in the neighbourhood.'

'Captain,' said Sita, as she got down from her horse, 'I will stay with you. Whatever fate awaits you, we will share it together...'

'Good!' said Corcoran with pleasure, 'that makes it all more straightforward. They're coming now, all the English, and John Robarts, and Barclay, and the colonels and the captains and the majors and all the red-jackets of creation.'

Corcoran searched the saddlebags of the two horses, and found two loaded revolvers, and there was a third in his belt, and cartridges in his pockets.

'We have enough weapons and ammunition,' he said, 'for

thirty or forty shots, and because I will only fire when I am sure of my target, I think all will go well in the end. Come with me, Sita. And Louison, you go ahead, like a scout, and make sure there are no enemies hiding in the jungle.'

Corcoran's plan was very simple. From the road where they were, he had spotted in the distance a small abandoned temple, at the end of a path leading into the jungle. They would seek sanctuary there. And so they went inside the temple and closed the door behind them. Corcoran began to barricade themselves in, using wood that was lying around, and made small holes in the door that he could fire through.

Louison watched these preparations with astonishment. She was a little gloomy, and wasn't able to understand what was happening. She loved the fresh air, the prairies, the vast forests, the high mountains. She didn't like to be locked up, and more particularly she couldn't understand why they were making such an effort to lock themselves up. So Corcoran carefully explained to her what they were doing.

'Louison, my dear,' he said, 'this is not the time to be capricious and run about in the fields as is your wretched habit... If you had done your duty this morning, we wouldn't, you and me, be shut up now, without having eaten, in this vile temple where there is not a morsel of fresh meat to be found. You were bad, my dear. You must make amends in a dramatic fashion. Now, pay attention! Hide behind that open window, and if any gentleman attempts to climb in, he's all yours, my dear.'

Having given these orders, which Louison promised to carry out promptly, or at least one could sense her keenness in this regard from the affectionate way in which she wagged her tail, and half opened her lips, Corcoran returned to Sita to give her encouragement.

'Oh, don't worry about reassuring me, Captain,' she said holding out her hand. 'It's not for my life that I fear. It's for you, who is going to give up your life so generously, and for my father who would not survive, I'm sure, the despair of seeing me in the hands of the English. But,' she added, her eyes brimming with pride, 'be sure that the daughter of Holkar will not be taken alive by these red-haired barbarians. I will either be free with you, or I will die.'

And she pulled from her belt a small flask which contained one of those subtle poisons that can be found everywhere in India.

'There,' she said, 'this will save me from servitude and the dishonour of marrying that traitor Rao.'

Just as she finished speaking, Corcoran heard a gentle noise like the hissing of the hooded cobra, the most terrifying snake in India. He got up quickly, but Sita gestured for him to sit down again.

The hissing was following by the hum of a hummingbird, and then the sound of leaves being crushed.

'What's that?' said Corcoran.

'There's nothing to fear. It's a friend,' replied Sita. 'I know that signal.'

And then, after a few moments, the voice of a man began chanting these words of the *Ramayana*, in which King Janaka of Videha presents his beautiful daughter Sita to Rama, her fiancé.

'I have a daughter, as beautiful as the goddesses, and endowed with every virtue; she is called Sita, and I have reserved her for the strongest of her suitors. So often, kings have come to ask for her in marriage, but I have responded to them: her hand in marriage is destined as a reward to the one who shows the greatest vigour…'

Sita got up, and recited, as a response to the question that came from outside the walls of the temple, the beautiful words that Sita spoke, in Valmiki's poem, to her husband, Rama, when, because of the perfidy of Kaikeyi, the invincible heroes were sent into exile and deprived of their throne.

'… Oh you, whose beautiful eyes are like lotus petals, why do I not see your fly-whisk and your fan surrounding your face, which is equal in splendour to the full circle of a night star?'

'Let me in!' shouted a voice from outside. 'Open up. It's me, Sugriva.'

Corcoran put his hand through the window, and when the Indian, climbing up the protrusions on the wall, was able to reach that hand, the powerful Breton pulled him up like a feather and sat him down on the floor of the temple.

He had hardly been in the temple a few seconds when he prostrated himself in front of Holkar's daughter.

'Get up,' said Sita. 'Where are the English?'

'Just five hundred paces from here.'

'Are they still looking for us?' asked Corcoran.

'Yes.'

'And have they been able to follow our trail?'

'Yes. One of the two horses you were riding was injured, hit by a bullet. They've concluded that you must be nearby.'

'And you, what is your plan?'

The Indian began to laugh silently.

'I blocked the road with the cart I was driving. The other coolies did the same. That gave you an extra quarter of an hour.'

At this point, Corcoran realised that Sugriva's face was bleeding.

'Who did that to you?'

'His Lordship, John Robarts,' replied the Indian. 'When he saw that the cart had overturned he struck me with his whip. But we will meet again. Oh yes, I will find him within three days, that dog of an Englishman.'

'Sugriva,' said the beautiful Sita, 'my father will give you the reward you so richly deserve…'

'Well,' said the Indian, 'I wouldn't give up my vengeance for all of Prince Holkar's treasure. I will have my vengeance soon, I know it.'

And, seeing a doubting look in the eyes of Corcoran, he said, 'Captain, you are one of us, since you are a friend of Holkar. Within three months there will not be a single Englishman in India.'

'Oh, really?' said Corcoran. 'I've already heard quite a few prophecies, and that one is no more certain than the others.'

'Believe me,' said Sugriva, 'all the sepoys of India have taken an oath to exterminate the English, and the massacre will start in five days' time in Meerut, Lahore and Benares.'

'How can you be sure?'

'I know it to be true. I am the confidential messenger of Nana Sahib, the Raja of Bithoor.'[27]

'But aren't you worried that I might warn the English?'

'It would be too late,' replied the Indian.

'But explain to me, then,' continued Corcoran, 'why have you come here?'

'Captain,' replied Sugriva, 'I will go wherever I can do harm to the English. And I do not want Robarts to die by any other hand than mine…'

Just then, Sugriva interrupted himself.

'I can hear the sound of horses trotting along the path,' he said. 'It's the English cavalry arriving. Steady yourselves, the assault is going to be pretty rough.'

'Good, good,' said Corcoran, 'this is hardly my first time. You, Sugriva, load the weapons, and you, Sita, pray for the protection of Brahma.'

A few moments later, fifty or sixty horsemen had surrounded the temple, and had their weapons at the ready. All the others had returned to the English camp.

Robarts, who was commanding the detachment, moved forward and said in a loud voice:

'Give yourself up, Captain, or you will die!'

'And if I give myself up,' replied Corcoran, 'will Holkar's daughter and I then be set free?'

'By the devil!' exclaimed Robarts, 'you are in our power. Do you think you can dictate terms? Give yourself up, and your life will be saved. There, that is all I can promise.'

'Oh really?' said Corcoran. 'Do as you please, then. I will do the same. And let battle commence.'

On hearing this, the English dismounted, tied their horses to the trees and got ready to break down the door of the temple with the butts of their rifles.

At the first strike of the first butt, the door shook and wobbled on its hinges.

'This is what you wanted,' said Corcoran, 'we are acting according to your wishes.'

And as he spoke, he fired his revolver through the half-open window.

An Englishman fell, mortally wounded.

Immediately, Corcoran pushed himself up against the wall, and no sooner had he done so than fifteen or twenty rifle shots came through the window. None of them hit him.

'You children,' he said, 'you're just throwing your gunpowder to the sparrows. This is how you should take aim.'

And with a second shot, he wounded one of the assailants.

After this, the English responded by opening fire again, which did Corcoran no more harm than before.

'Gentlemen,' he said, 'you're doing nothing more than breaking the windows. Aren't you going to try something more serious?'

That was certainly the intention of the English.

While most of them were continuing to fire at the door and window of the temple, five or six of the English horsemen went off to find a tree trunk, and soon carried one back in triumph.

'What the devil! This is becoming serious,' thought Corcoran.

He turned to Sugriva and said: 'They are going to break down the door; that's clear. And that will lead to a full-scale assault. Nobody knows what might happen. Take Sita to a corner of the temple where you can shelter her from the bullets.'

Sita, full of admiration for Corcoran's bravery, wanted to remain beside him, but Sugriva led her away and made her hide in a corner.

During all this time, Louison said nothing.

This intelligent beast understood all the wishes and all the thoughts of Corcoran. She knew that she had been given the task of guarding the window, and nothing would distract her from that duty. And so, following orders, she was silent, lying flat on her stomach, her paws extended, thinking and waiting.

Meanwhile, the tree trunk was brought with great fanfare towards the door of the temple. With the first blow, the door did not give way. But with the second blow, one part of the door was broken, and left a gap almost large enough for a man to enter.

Corcoran saw this immediate danger, and leaving Louison to guard the window, he ran to the breach in the door. He was just in time, because a red-haired Englishman was already visible and trying to get his shoulders through the breach. Fortunately, the gap was still a little too narrow.

When the Englishman saw Corcoran approaching, he tried to open fire with his rifle, but because he was trapped in the broken door he couldn't get into position to take aim. Corcoran, on the other hand, was free from such constraints – the master of his own movements. He placed the muzzle of his revolver against the skull of the Englishman, and blew his brains out.

Then, since he was running out of ammunition, he dragged the body of the Englishman inside, took his rifle and his cartridges, and still more precious, a flask of eau-de-vie of which he had great need.

That done, he closed the breach by placing the body of the Englishman in front of the door. Then he waited.

The English were becoming impatient.

They had not expected to come up against such serious resistance. They had already suffered two deaths, and one injury, and they feared more losses.

'What if we set fire to the temple?' suggested a lieutenant.

Fortunately, John Robarts didn't agree.

'Colonel Barclay,' he pointed out, 'promised us ten thousand pounds sterling if we bring him Holkar's daughter alive. So we have nothing to gain if she dies. Come on. One more effort, my boys! Can a Frenchman really defeat old England? If we can't get in through the door, let's try the window!'

And that's what they did. While half the troops continued to fire at the door, the rest of them headed to the window which was about twelve feet away. Three or four soldiers gave one of the sergeants a leg-up. He put his hand on the edge of the window and, with a great show of strength, was able to pull himself up, and managed to sit on the window frame.

Seeing him there, his comrades shouted, 'Hurrah.'

But the poor devil did not even have the time to respond to them. Before he could open his mouth, Louison stood up on her hind legs, placed her front paws on the window frame, and with her teeth seized the unfortunate sergeant by the neck, breaking it, and tossing the body out of the window on top of his terrified comrades.

Until then, they had forgotten about Louison. And the exploits of the tiger rapidly cooled the ardour of the horsemen.

'Anyway,' asked one of the officers, 'what are we doing here? We should be back at camp. If Barclay lets Holkar's daughter escape, then it's for him to sort out and recapture her if he can… There are about fifty of us here, busy taking potshots at a gentleman whom we don't know, who has done us no harm, and wouldn't harm us if we agreed to leave him alone. Frankly, there's no sense to what we are doing.'

'Barclay wants to recapture Holkar's daughter,' said John

Robarts, 'and Barclay must have his reasons. And so I am not leaving until I have completed my mission.'

'Oh well,' replied the officer, 'there's no hurry, I suppose. We can capture Holkar's daughter and her protector more easily and more comfortably tomorrow. Night is coming. We need to set up a proper guard, weapons at the ready. And then we can dine and sleep. Corcoran has no food. Soon, he will be forced to surrender.'

This calculation was correct enough, and Corcoran, who heard this discussion, was worried for the future.

He watched the English soldiers draw back a little from the temple, keeping it still in view. They deployed sentries at regular intervals, and sat down to dinner. The Indian coolies had followed them from a distance with their wagons, and were unpacking the silverware, venison pâtés, cold meat and bottles of claret.

The sight of this redoubled Corcoran's feelings of hunger, and made his belly squirm. He had hardly had any breakfast, and the day had been so full of incident that he had not stopped for a moment to think about eating.

But this was nothing compared to the worry he felt for his dear Sita, brought up in the luxury and abundance of a palace, and suddenly finding herself reduced to the most extreme fatigue and hunger.

And even more worrying was Louison. Certainly, the tigress was a devoted friend, but her appetite was even greater than her devotion.

And who could reproach her? Isn't the stomach, according to the physiologists, the master and sovereign of all nature? How could one reproach a poor tiger, barely exposed to civilisation, for not being mistress of her passions and her appetite? Especially, when one sees, every day, the great princes, raised with care by learned teachers and nourished since infancy by the wisdom of the philosophers, lack, in such a striking fashion, all precepts of morality and philosophy.

Corcoran was worried, and with good reason, for the future. He saw the eyes of Louison turn covetously towards the unfortunate Sugriva, and he feared an irreparable accident.

However, there wasn't much of a choice of victims, since Louison clearly wanted to eat at any cost, and she had become agitated, leaping about purposelessly. Obviously, she was very hungry.

Finally, Corcoran accepted the inevitable.

'By my faith,' he thought, 'it's better that she eats an Englishman than that she doesn't eat at all, or that she eats my poor friend Sugriva.'

With that thought, he called out to the Indian.

'Are you hungry?' asked Corcoran.

'Yes, I am.'

'Have you got any food?'

'No.'

'Do you want to have dinner?

Sugriva looked at him as if he didn't understand.

'Yes, now listen carefully,' said Corcoran, 'you want to know where the dinner is. Well, look…'

And with his hand, he showed Sugriva how the English were already sitting down on a carpet and had begun to eat.

'My friend,' continued Corcoran, 'Louison will go out there, and grab one of the guards. The others will shout. They will come running with their weapons. You will slip unseen through the grass, and take their dinner and bring it back here as quickly as possible. Do you understand now? And if necessary, I will come out, well-armed, to make sure you can return safely. Is that agreed?'

'It's agreed,' said the Brahmin.

Louison in turn received her instructions, which Corcoran gave her in a low voice, more with gestures than with words. The tigress anyway was so clever that she worked out immediately what her purpose was in leaving the temple, and she happily sneaked out of the half-open door and was followed by Sugriva.

The English were not expecting an attack, given their large numerical advantage. They were off-guard and drinking merrily. The moon, which had already risen, made all their movements clearly visible.

The sentry who was guarding the main door stood about ten paces away. In two leaps, Louison jumped on him, knocked his weapon away with a swipe of her paw, and bit deep into his head.

On hearing the scream of the dying sentry, all the English soldiers took up their arms and went to search for the enemy. But the sight of Louison made even the bravest of them stop for a moment. Meanwhile, Sugriva, who was almost naked, as is the custom of the Indians, profited from the disorder and the darkness, slid on his stomach to the spot where they had been feasting, and quickly gathered some bread, meat and a few bottles of wine, and returned without being seen.

To distract the English, Corcoran fired twice from the window without harming anyone. The English responded with at least forty rifle shots, every one of which hit the wall of the temple. Meanwhile, Sugriva had managed to run back

The English sentry stood guard

almost fifty paces to the temple door, and to slip through the opening with his booty.

The plan had succeeded admirably, except that Louison did not want to return. It was in vain that the Captain made his usual whistling sound. Louison was hanging on to her dead Englishman and did not want to let go.

The other Englishmen fired at her, but only at a distance and in darkness, because none of them dared to go up close in the night to such a fearsome adversary. Corcoran shuddered. Apart from the mutual feelings of tenderness that united him with Louison, he depended so much on her for his safety.

11

The end of the siege

There were a few moments of painful anxiety for Corcoran. Louison had let out a muffled roar when she was being fired on, and then lay flat on her stomach. Was she dead or wounded? Or was she just pretending in order to give her enemies a false sense of security. Corcoran looked out of the window and could see nothing. And the situation wasn't very reassuring for the English either. Standing in a large circle around the temple, five or six paces from each other, they reloaded their rifles, ready to fire again.

Suddenly there was a cry of distress that echoed through the silence of the night. Louison, creeping through the shadows, had broken through the line of soldiers, and knocked one of them over. She then dug her teeth deep into the Englishman's thigh, carrying him back to the temple in her mouth.

Corcoran went to the door and made Louison let go of her prey, sure that no one would dare fire just then, for fear of wounding or killing the man she had been carrying. He got Louison to re-enter the temple, and in doing so set the unfortunate Englishman free.

But the poor devil wasn't very sensitive to the generosity of the victor, since his thigh had been shredded by the teeth of a tigress, and he had fainted.

'Messieurs,' shouted Corcoran after having taken the man's rifle, his revolver and ammunition, 'you can come and get your friend. He is only injured.'

'Dog of a Frenchman!' exclaimed John Robarts, who sent two men to find their injured companion, and carry him to safety, 'are your weapons and your allies worthy of a gentleman?'

'But, you dog of an Englishman,' replied Corcoran, 'there are fifty or sixty of you against me. And why have you come to shoot me, when I only ask for peace with you and with the entire world?'

As he spoke, he repaired the breach in the door, and piled up, with the help of Sugriva, anything that would help serve as a barricade.

'Now let us see,' said Corcoran, 'if the wine of these heretics is any good. It's claret… Thanks be to Brahma and Vishnu! I feared that it would be a bottle of pale ale made by Mr Allsopp.[28] God be praised! The pâté is excellent. Eat, Sita! And you, Sugriva. Finish it up. Tomorrow morning we will either be killed or rescued.'

'Captain,' said Sugriva, 'there's some cause for hope. I have just made a discovery.'

'What?'

'Just now, while looking for some wood to stick in that cursed hole they made in the door, I felt a trapdoor beneath my feet. Captain, that trapdoor must lead to a tunnel, and that tunnel must emerge somewhere in the countryside. If that's so we will be saved.'

'Saved, you say? Yes, you will be saved, but not Sita. You can see that the poor child is exhausted, and is in no state to walk anywhere.'

'My Lord, if I find the tunnel as I found the trapdoor, and if the tunnel ends, as I hope, in open countryside, I will be able to inform Holkar this very night. And he will be able to come to our rescue.'

Corcoran got up immediately.

Sugriva wasn't wrong. Behind the altar of Vishnu was a trapdoor and under the trapdoor, which he was only able to open with some difficulty, was a staircase with twenty steps.

'You go down the stairs,' said Corcoran, 'and I will watch you from here.'

Fortunately, Corcoran had a small tinder-box, and he lit one of the candles from the altar. Sugriva took it and descended slowly. After a few minutes he returned.

'The tunnel is like a corridor,' he said, 'and it ends in a gate, about one hundred paces away, beyond where the English are camping. I am certain I can get to Bhagavpur so long as there are no tigers prowling about.'

'Remember,' said Corcoran, 'that though it is peaceful now in the night, the morning will be stormy – so tell Holkar to make haste.'

'Sugriva,' said the beautiful Sita, 'tell my father, Holkar, that his daughter is well-guarded by the bravest and most generous of men. And you, Captain, sleep a little; it's my turn to watch over you...'

Sugriva prostrated himself, lifted his hands up in the shape of a cup, and left.

Corcoran, alone with Holkar's daughter, sat next to her and said, 'Dear Sita, I will remember for a long time the good fortune I have had this evening of being close to you…'

'My Lord Corcoran,' replied the princess, 'it feels now as if I have always lived like this, and my previous life, so peaceful and quiet, was only a dream compared to all that I have seen and felt today.'

'And what did you feel?' asked the Breton.

'I don't know,' she responded innocently. 'I was frightened. I thought they wanted to kill me. I thought that I would kill myself in order to escape the infamous Rao. When I saw you in the English camp, I once again felt some hope, and I was sure of it when I witnessed the courage and coolness with which you braved all of these dangers.'

Corcoran smiled as he listened to these innocent words.

'What a charming girl!' he thought, and that it was so much better to spend the night in this temple in peaceful conversation about Brahma, Shiva and Vishnu (despite the presence of the English and their rifles), than on a foolish search for the original manuscript of the *Guru Karamta*, on behalf of the Academy of Sciences of Lyon… 'Ah! There is nothing in the world quite as good as saving beautiful princesses, or even giving one's life for them.'

With these thoughts, Corcoran felt a drowsiness overcome him. The danger didn't seem so great now, because the English were also exhausted.

Meanwhile, Louison watched over them, or if she slept it was just with one eye, as cats, her domestic cousins, do; and her other eye, half-open, could still make out small objects in the thick darkness. And as an alternative to her eyes, her ears also listened out for the smallest sound.

That's why, seeing that all was tranquil, and that Sita had also succumbed to fatigue, Corcoran stretched out on a mat and slept until daybreak.

12

Give me that Englishman! What do you want to do with him? Hang him! Most willingly!

While everyone inside and outside the temple was sleeping, apart from Louison and the two sentries, Sugriva made his way along the underground corridor and reached a locked gate. But he could find no way of opening it.

He searched for a long time for some means by which he could open the gate, and eventually, by fumbling around, he pushed with his foot against a small limbless statue of Brahma supporting the universe on his shoulders.

The statue creaked slightly, turned around, and the gate opened. Sugriva immediately put out the candle, silently closed the gate behind him and slid through the bushes.

He had a plan. He carefully looked round the camp – where the English soldiers were sleeping without a care, relying on the vigilance of the two sentries.

As Sugriva crawled like a snake through the jungle, he was

noticed by one of the Indian coolies. The latter was about to sound the alarm, but Sugriva made a secret sign with two raised fingers of his right hand.

The other man kept silent.

Sugriva was searching for two things: a horse, so that he could deliver his message to Holkar, and John Robarts, so he could chop off his head.

Fortunately for Robarts, he was fast asleep next to a half-lit tent, in the midst of ten or twelve other gentlemen, whose legs and arms were all entangled in the most picturesque fashion.

Sugriva had spotted his enemy; but if he tried to kill him, the entire camp would wake up and his mission would fail. He decided, for the moment, to be patient, promising himself that one day soon he would return for John Robarts.

He carefully unhitched one of the horses which had been loosely tied to a nearby tree, bridled it and, in order to avoid making a noise, wrapped its hooves in pieces of felt he found nearby. Then he slowly made his way from the camp, leading the horse by its bridle.

During this time the coolie, who had not lost sight of him, came up and asked him in a low voice:

'On which day will it happen?'

'Soon,' responded Sugriva.

'Where are you going?'

'To Holkar's camp.'

'Shall I come with you?'

'There's no point. Stay here. When I need help, I will tell you. The big event will happen in a week.'

'Shiva be praised!' replied the Indian.

He returned to the camp, and lay down peacefully next to his comrades, while Sugriva, climbing on to his saddle, departed, slowly at first, then at a slow trot, and when he believed he was far enough away from the English, at a great gallop, heading towards Bhagavpur.

Thank heavens he didn't have an accident on the way and he did not meet a soul.

All the inhabitants of the villages situated between the English camp and Bhagavpur had abandoned their houses because they were expecting a great battle. They feared pillage, or murder, or fire, and all those other great exploits which occur habitually during war, and which mark the lives of heroes.

As soon as Sugriva arrived at an outpost of Bhagavpur, he was met with curiosity. 'Before anything,' he insisted, 'where is Holkar?'

They took him to the palace.

The unfortunate Prince was half-sitting, half-lying on a carpet, and was asleep. Since the abduction of his daughter, he had only one thought, and in his despair he came close to stabbing himself, but the desire for vengeance still sustained him.

'Who is there?' he said as he lifted his weary head. 'What new misfortune have you come to tell me about?'

'Lord Holkar,' said the messenger, 'do you remember me? I am Sugriva, friend of Tantia Tope and of you'.

'Ah, yes! Tantia Tope. He will arrive too late! And where have you come from, Sugriva?'

'From the English camp.'

'You have seen the English!' exclaimed Holkar, reanimated by anger. 'Where are they? What are they doing? It is because of them that I have lost my daughter, my poor Sita!'

Great tears ran down the cheeks of the old man.

'My Lord,' said Sugriva, 'your daughter has been found.'

'Where is she? In the hands of Colonel Barclay, or the infamous Rao?'

'She is in safety, my Lord, at least for the moment. That brave Frenchman, your guest, found her, and is guarding her.'

Sugriva briefly told him the story of how Corcoran and Sita escaped.

'There is not a moment to lose if we are to rescue them,' he said finally. 'Tomorrow morning the English will get reinforcements, and then there would have to be a great battle and success would be far from certain.'

'Fine,' said Holkar. 'Call Ali!'

Ali, who was watching from behind the door, his sword unsheathed, entered the room.

'Ali,' said the Prince, 'sound the call-to-arms for the cavalry. Everyone must be ready to leave in half an hour.'

In the blink of an eye, the order was given, and trumpets were sounded in the streets of the city. The horsemen gathered, and Holkar's favourite elephant was hurriedly harnessed.

'This is the elephant Sita most likes to ride,' explained her poor father. 'You, Sugriva, take a horse, and be our guide.'

'My Lord,' said the Indian, 'I hope you will grant me a favour in exchange for the service I am rendering you.'

'Ten favours, one hundred, one thousand! Half of all my land if you can bring back my daughter,' exclaimed Holkar.

'No, my Lord, I don't have such ambitions. What I would like is the life of Lieutenant John Robarts.'

'You want to save the life of that foreigner?'

'Me?' exclaimed Sugriva, with a wild laugh. 'Save him? Never! Let me never see Vishnu again, should I even think of saving an Englishman.'

'Then, that's easy,' said Holkar. 'I will give him to you, and ten others as well.'

As they prepared to depart, Holkar questioned Sugriva about the strength and location of the English army.

'My Lord,' said the Indian, 'I know everything. The day before yesterday, in the evening, I left Bhagavpur to visit the 21st Sepoy Regiment, in which I have friends and spies. Because I was dressed as a beggar none of the red-jackets bothered me. They let me wander freely through their camp, and I was even able to recite my prayers to Vishnu. And I spoke to several soldiers, of whom one is a sergeant and part of our conspiracy.

'My Lord, it was a pleasure to see how much the cursed English are hated and distrusted... Everything about them is horrible. Their blasphemies, their greed, their custom of eating sacred food, their impiety, the sermons of their priests, the brutality of their leaders, the severity of their discipline. Can you believe, my Lord, that they whip Brahmins, men of high caste, as if they were young children...?

'So, in a few hours,' Sugriva continued, 'I was able to learn everything I needed, and had given my orders to everyone. I was just leaving when I saw Princess Sita, your daughter, arrive in the camp, brought there by the traitor Rao.'

On hearing this, Holkar sighed deeply, and said, 'When I think that I had that miserable man at my feet, and could have just had him impaled there and then, and I didn't do it! So, let us leave now!'

Holkar climbed on to the saddle of his horse and set off at a fast trot, followed by two regiments of cavalry.

Since the distance which separated Bhagavpur and the temple where Corcoran was under siege was hardly three leagues, Holkar arrived at the battlefield a little after daybreak.

13

The Captain's toilette

By five o'clock in the morning, the chill of the night had woken everyone – and Corcoran first of all.

He got up, loaded his weapons carefully, and then went straight to the window where Louison was still lying down, half-awake and half-asleep. Corcoran stretched his arms while yawning and looked out at the horizon.

There wasn't a cloud in the sky. A few stars were still sparkling their last, and then they disappeared. The moon had already set.

The only sound that he could hear in the entire countryside was the rushing water of a rocky stream some distance away.

All nature seemed at peace, and for their part the Englishmen, now slowly stretching their arms, seemed to have no desire to fight. Except for the fiery John Robarts, who thought otherwise.

This gentleman had dreamed all night of the ten thousand pounds sterling promised by Colonel Barclay. He had somewhere, in Scotland perhaps, others said it was in

England – yes, it was England, I remember now, just three leagues away from Canterbury – an aunt who was red-haired and ugly.

But that aunt who was red-haired and ugly had a daughter who was blond and pretty, the first cousin of John Robarts – Miss Julia. And this cousin played the piano. Oh yes, she played the piano with such talent. And it is such a pleasure to listen to pretty girls playing the piano.

But let us return to the cousin of John Robarts. Miss Julia sang the most admirable songs, romantic songs in which the moon, little birds, doves, clouds, smiles and tears all play a prominent role – as they do in our most admirable French romantic songs – and which made her think all day about the red whiskers of John Robarts, who, in turn, thinks three times a week about the blue eyes of Julia.

And out of these thoughts was born, as one might expect, a mutual sympathy.

But because Miss Julia had inherited fifteen thousand pounds sterling, and because Mrs Robarts, John's aunt, was good at calculations, and because she knew that John didn't have a single shilling apart from his pay – in fact he owed five or six hundred pounds sterling to his bootmaker, his tailor, his tassel-maker and his other suppliers – John couldn't get beyond the entrance of the delightful cottage where Miss Julia spent her days in the company of her mother.

Out of desperation, John asked to be sent to India, where he hoped to make his fortune like Clive, Hastings and all the other nabobs.[29]

He was granted this favour, thanks to the intervention of Sir William[30] Barrowlinson, Baronet, of whom we have already spoken, and who was one of the directors of the East India Company.

But although John Robarts was very brave, he hadn't yet had the opportunity to demonstrate his bravery, and he now wished that all of India was on fire, so that he, Robarts, would have the pleasure of stamping out the fire, and equalling the glory of Arthur Wellesley, Duke of Wellington.[31] And that's why he fought, day and night, with so much passion, hoping always to find the fortune necessary to buy the delightful cottage near Canterbury – Robarts House – and with that cottage, the young proprietress.

And that's the reason why he kept pursuing Corcoran and Sita so passionately.

Robarts was also up and about at the same time as Corcoran.

'Come on, get up,' he said, 'you lazybones! Inglis! Whitworth! Get up! The sun has risen. Barclay will be waiting for us and we don't want to return to the camp empty-handed.'

Thanks to Robarts everyone was soon awake.

Each of them washed in their customary manner. They had brought travelling-cases with all sorts of combs and brushes, soaps and perfumes and they performed their ablutions in the open air, where Corcoran was able to see them.

This spectacle, which should have cheered up the Breton, put him in a worse temper.

Aren't they lucky, these *goddams*,' he thought, 'to be able to wash themselves as usual, and make themselves ready to appear before a lady? As for me, upon my word, I am about as well-turned-out as a mud-covered dog. My clothes are covered with dust, my hair is entangled like the sentences of a Balzac novel, and I must have the gaunt, pale, exhausted look of someone who

John Robarts prepares for combat

is either scared to death or bored out of their mind. Sita will wake up soon at the sound of rifle shots, and if by misfortune I am killed, her last memory of me will be of a great scarecrow. But what can I do? How can I avoid this misfortune?'

He stared tenderly at Sita for some time.

'How beautiful she is!' he said to himself. 'She dreams, no doubt, that she is in her father's palace, and that she has a hundred servants at her command. Poor Sita! And who could have said to me just the day before yesterday that I would have been willing to give my life for a woman. Perhaps I am in love with her… Bah! What is the point of all that? I'd be better off searching peacefully for the manuscript of the *Guru Karamta*.'

Suddenly, as he looked out of the window, an idea came to him.

The English had already finished their ablutions, and were putting their combs and brushes back in their travelling-cases, when Corcoran pulled his white handkerchief out of his pocket and used it to signal to the guard that he should come closer.

The guard came up to the window.

'Please call Mr John Robarts,' said Corcoran, 'I have an important request to make of him.'

John Robarts approached joyfully, believing the ten thousand pounds sterling was now his.

'So, Captain,' he said with an air of triumph, 'you wish to surrender? I knew that you would do so, sooner or later. And I won't force you to accept terms that are too harsh. Simply open the door, hand over Holkar's daughter and then follow us. I am sure that Barclay will set you free, and only ask that you return to Europe. At heart, Barclay is a good sort.'

Corcoran smiled.

'By my faith,' he said, 'my dear Robarts, I'd be happy to deal with you in such circumstances, you and Barclay, but I don't think it's quite got to that stage for the moment. Now, I notice that you have brought with you all your toiletries, running water, servants to polish your boots and clean your clothes. Would you be so good as to lend me…?'

'By Jove,' said John Robarts, for whom adventure should always be congenial, 'whatever you want.'

And he handed the Captain his wash-bag.

'And as for your surrender…?' he added.

'Ah, yes, well…' said Corcoran, 'I would like a truce for a quarter of an hour to reflect and take a decision.'

'Nothing could be more reasonable,' responded the Englishman, 'and look, Captain, I like you. I don't quite know why I like you, since last night you let your tiger eat one of my best friends. Poor old Waddington.'

'You know,' replied Corcoran, 'it wasn't my fault that Louison ate him up. The poor beast had gone without dinner.'

'Give yourselves up,' said Robarts. 'We won't do you any harm, nor to Holkar's daughter. Do you think we would fight a war against women? Would the French fight a war against women?'

'My dear Robarts,' said the Breton, 'don't waste time on such conversations during the quarter of an hour truce that you have agreed.'

Robarts moved away. Immediately, Corcoran began to wash, which he did very quickly, because he feared that the English, whom he was watching closely, might try to surprise him.

But his fears were unjustified. There was no attempt at treachery.

Now he was ready. He looked at his watch – the fifteen minutes had expired. He wanted, at least, to say a final goodbye to Holkar's daughter.

As he approached her she opened her eyes.

'Where am I?' she asked with a look of astonishment. Then, seeing the temple and remembering the events of the previous day, she said, 'Ah, my dream couldn't have been better. I was in Bhagavpur, on the throne of my father… you were at my side.'

'Sita, dear Sita, I am certain that Sugriva has kept his promise and your father will come to rescue us. He should be here soon, but if something happens to me, an accident perhaps...'

'Oh don't talk like that, Corcoran, I am sure you will be victorious. That's what I dreamed, and dreams never lie.'

'Ah well,' said Corcoran, 'promise me that you will always remember me.'

'I promise,' said Sita, 'that I…'

She stopped herself, and began to blush.

'…that I will never forget you.'

Corcoran, who feared that he was becoming soft-hearted, ran to the window.

Robarts was already getting impatient.

'Well, Captain,' he said, 'the truce is over, and the show is about to begin. We must be back in our camp by ten in the morning, and it is already six.'

'I am ready,' shouted Corcoran.

And indeed he was ready, just about, since he managed to step aside and avoid a hail of bullets which were fired in his direction. The bullets hit the walls of the temple without hurting anyone.

But because the English, to get into position, had come out into the open, Corcoran was able to take aim at Robarts, and fired. The bullet made a hole in Robarts' hat and removed a lock of his hair.

Robarts retreated instinctively and took shelter behind a nearby tree.

'You see, my friend,' shouted Corcoran from the window, 'it is necessary to aim carefully when you get caught up in a battle; I only wanted to make a hole in your hat.'

This was soon followed by a tragic incident which failed to end the assault, and which resulted in the enemy entering the temple.

One of the Englishmen tried to get into the temple through the breach in the doorway that had been made the previous day, and which Corcoran, lacking suitable materials, had been unable to barricade properly. If the Englishman got through the breach, he would have been able to put an immediate end to the battle by striking Corcoran from behind.

Fortunately, Louison had woken up. Hidden behind part of the door, she waited for the Englishman. He pushed at the barricade, removing two or three planks which weren't properly secured, and managed to get halfway into the temple. But the tigress knocked him over with one blow from his paw, and bit his throat so savagely that he died immediately.

This sight, and the taste of blood, only increased Louison's appetite. She would probably have sacrificed the pleasure of battle to the pleasure of eating, if Corcoran hadn't whistled and sent her back to her post.

Corcoran was beginning to be worried. There was no news of Holkar. He wondered if Sugriva had been able to complete his mission. And he was running out of ammunition.

When Corcoran appeared briefly at the window, he was a target for forty or forty-five rifles, whose covering fire protected those who were now charging at the temple door with the battering ram. The hinges were already half broken, and it was about to give way entirely.

Corcoran, moving across the opening, fired five revolver shots at the mass of attackers. From the curses he heard, he could tell that he had been on target, but his overall position had not improved.

'Quickly, run up[32] the staircase!' he shouted at Sita. 'There's nothing to be afraid of.'

She obeyed, and Corcoran followed her. Louison was the rearguard.

Soon, the temple door burst open with a huge crash, and through the open breach poured all the attackers at the same time.

But they were hugely surprised when they saw only Louison on the staircase. From behind her came the sound of Corcoran's revolver, firing from the shadows, but the winding staircase hid him from view.

'Goddamn,' exclaimed Robarts in fury, 'not another siege. Give yourselves up, Captain. Resistance is impossible'.

'The word impossible does not exist in French.'

'If we take you by force, you will be shot.'

'So be it, shoot me then!' said the Breton. 'And if I capture you, then I will cut off your ears.'

'Prepare arms!' shouted Robarts.

The soldiers obeyed him.

'Dear Sita,' said Corcoran, 'go further up the staircase,

The siege of the staircase

please, several more steps, a bullet might bounce off the wall and hit you.'

Corcoran also went up the stairs, and was soon followed by Louison. In that way, thanks to the manner in which the staircase had been constructed, they were able to find shelter from the bullets. And if it was a matter of hand-to-hand combat in such a confined space, all the advantage would be with Corcoran and Louison.

But another unexpected event changed everything.

An English soldier, who had remained outside to prevent Corcoran's escape, ran hurriedly inside the temple screaming, 'The enemy is here.'

'What enemy?' asked Robarts. 'Surely, it must be Colonel Barclay sending reinforcements.'

'No, it's Holkar. I saw the flags.'

Now they could hear the heavy gallop of cavalry.

'What the devil!' thought Robarts. 'That's ten thousand pounds sterling just thrown away, quite apart from what Holkar will do to us.'

And at the top of his voice he said, 'Everyone out. And mount your horses.'

All his soldiers hurriedly obeyed him.

'And now,' said Robarts, 'with sword in hand let us charge that rabble. Attack in the name of old England!'

And he moved at a fast trot in the direction of Holkar's forces.

14

How the besiegers became the besieged

Even though the two forces were unequal in terms of numbers, the outcome of the battle was finely balanced.

Moreover, the English cavalry, composed entirely of Europeans, was far superior to Holkar's cavalry in man-to-man fighting, and the lie of the land did not allow Holkar to encircle the English and make use of his numerical advantage.

The temple had been built on high ground, in the midst of thick jungle, which could not be entered on horseback. Three paths had been cut through the jungle, each leading to the high ground. The paths were all pretty straight, and easy to defend. Once Holkar's horsemen reached these paths, they found themselves face-to-face with the English – and victory would depend more on individual courage than on the number of fighters.

Holkar shuddered when he saw the problems posed by the difficult terrain.

And the first clash between the two cavalries did not give Holkar much confidence of victory. His men held firm quite well when the English began firing on them from a distance. But when they saw the English – John Robarts at their head – advancing rapidly towards them, swords unsheathed, ready to cut them to pieces, nothing could stop them from fleeing.

Holkar's horsemen simply turned round and rode back in the direction of Bhagavpur. But on the way, Holkar was able to rally them again, telling them how the English were outnumbered – and this bolstered their confidence and courage.

John Robarts, carried away by his own ardour, tried to push home his advantage by following the enemy. But on arriving at the main road, on the edge of a vast plain where Holkar could easily surround them, he changed his plans, and the English retreated at a slow trot, with Holkar now following them in slow pursuit.

Sugriva came up to Holkar.

'I don't understand,' said Holkar, 'is Corcoran dead, or has he been taken prisoner with my daughter?'

'My Lord,' said Sugriva, 'I will try to find out. One thing is certain, your daughter is still alive, because the English have been trying so hard to capture her that they wouldn't touch a hair on her head, and as for the Captain, I've seen him in action, and the bullet that would kill him hasn't been made yet.'

As he finished speaking, there was a lot of shouting by the English soldiers. Corcoran was escaping from the temple, preceded by Louison and the beautiful Sita.

When Corcoran saw that the English were leaving the temple, he had little doubt that Holkar had arrived, but because he had so little confidence in the courage of the unhappy

Indians, he didn't feel sure of being rescued. But before attempting to escape he wanted to consult Sita.

'We're only about five hundred paces away from your father,' he said. 'Should we take the risk of trying to join up with him, no matter what?'

In response, Sita said she was ready to follow Corcoran.

'Pay careful attention,' continued Corcoran. 'The battle has started, and the bullets are flying. I'm going to send Louison ahead along the left-hand path, which is barely guarded. And when the five or six horsemen who are there see Louison, they will run away, you can be sure of it. Now, you follow Louison, and I will follow you.'

And so, profiting from the distraction in the English ranks caused by Holkar's arrival, the three of them crossed the open space that separated them from the jungle, then made their way through some bushes and, guided by the sound of gunfire, were able to find their way, safe and sound, to Holkar and his cavalry.

On seeing his daughter again, Holkar, full of joy, hugged her tightly, and turned to Corcoran.

'Oh Captain,' he said, 'how can I ever repay you for what you have done?'

'Lord Holkar,' replied the Breton, 'as soon as you have some free time, I hope you will help me search for the famous manuscript of the *Guru Karamta* which the Academy of Sciences of Lyon is making such a fuss about, but today we have other business to sort out. If you want my view, I think we should retreat towards Bhagavpur. The main English army must be marching there right now, under the command of Colonel Barclay; it wouldn't take long for a more energetic commander to cut off our retreat. You should leave, and quickly!'

'And you?' asked Holkar.

'Me? That's another matter. Now, if you leave me one of your two regiments, I promise you that I will trap John Robarts inside the temple, and smoke him out like a fox. He wanted to shoot me, that gentleman! Well, I'm going to teach him a lesson.'

This idea was very pleasing to Holkar.

'But Captain,' he said to Corcoran, 'maybe you should accompany Sita, while I cut the throat of John Robarts.'

'On any other occasion I would accompany Sita with pleasure, but not today. Robarts provoked me, and I will deal with him.'

'Fine,' said Holkar, 'but I will be at your side.'

'I think,' added Corcoran, 'that you should also send some scouts in the direction of the English, so that you'll know when they're coming.' And so Sugriva, with about thirty horsemen, was charged with surveying the movements of the enemy.

'And Sita,' added Corcoran, 'should stay inside the palanquin on top of the elephant, and she must be properly defended and kept out of the range of bullets, and well away from that cursed Robarts.'

Inspired by the example of Holkar and the Captain, who were leading from the front, the Indian soldiers advanced with real pride towards their meeting with the enemy, which, in turn, was retreating.

Soon after the appearance of Holkar, Robarts had sent a soldier to warn Colonel Barclay of the dangers they were facing. Because as soon as he saw that Corcoran had escaped, he realised that his own position had become perilous. And so, without waiting to being forced inside, John Robarts and his soldiers sought sanctuary in the temple which had served as Corcoran's fortress.

They repaired as well as they could the breach they themselves had made earlier – fixing the door, piling up all the moveable objects they could find in order to barricade themselves in.

When Holkar's soldiers appeared, forty-three English rifles were pointing through the gun holes. They opened fire. There were several deaths and ten injured among the Indians, and this early setback dampened their ardour.

'I promise a thousand rupees,' said Holkar, 'to the first of you to set foot inside the temple.'

But no one was tempted by this offer. The unfortunate Indians realised that they were exposed, without shelter, to heavy gunfire. And the enemy's position, on the other hand, was well defended.

'Well,' said Corcoran to Holkar, 'clearly we will have to set an example, because your poor devils are scared of seeing Brahma and Vishnu face-to-face inside the temple.'

Corcoran dismounted, and followed by twenty others, picked up the tree trunk that the English had used as a battering ram. It crashed against the door of the temple, which gave way and fell backwards over the barricade that had been built up behind it.

Seeing this, there was a cry of joy from the Indians. But that joy was short-lived, because the English rifles were once again being aimed at the attackers, and this time, because they were so close, even the bravest of them didn't dare enter the temple.

Corcoran, seeing their hesitation, hurriedly ordered Holkar's soldiers to open fire, just as the English soldiers were doing the same – and a cloud of smoke soon enveloped them all. Five of the English had fallen, dead or dying. Ten or twelve Indians had met the same fate. The rest of them, discouraged by this stalemate, were visibly planning to retreat. Even Holkar himself was not sure what to do.

'Ah! If only…' thought the Breton, sighing, 'if only I had two or three good sailors from *The Son of the Tempest* with me, then we could attack immediately. But with these wet chickens there's not much to be done.'

'Well,' he said to Holkar, 'if only you had brought a cannon with you.'

'But why,' asked Holkar, 'don't we set fire to the temple? How about that?'

'I would have loved,' said Corcoran, 'to capture that badly brought-up gentleman alive, the one who wanted to have me shot… But since there's no other way, let's roast him.'

The Indians went off to cut dry grass, and pile it up around the temple. But at the moment when they were about to set it alight, they heard several rifle shots in the distance.

Hearing this noise, Corcoran and Holkar stopped and listened.

'Let's forget about these Englishmen and your vengeance,' said the Breton, 'and let's return as fast as we can to Bhagavpur. That firing must be the vanguard of Barclay's army.'

Holkar gave the order to turn around at once, to head for the main road, and to prepare for battle.

15

How Louison lay down like a cat at the feet of Sita as they both rode on the back of Scindia the elephant

Sugriva didn't take long to reappear, hotly pursued by Colonel Barclay's vanguard.

Barclay, who was already marching on Bhagavpur, had learnt, with a mixture of astonishment and indignation, of the danger that threatened Robarts, and was leading his cavalry in an attempt to rescue his lieutenant.

Sugriva, in trying to resist the headlong charge of the English, had lost half of his soldiers, and was only able to rejoin Holkar with great difficulty, since the English attacked him incessantly.

But when the English saw Holkar's two regiments holding their ground in battle formation, the spirit of Barclay's cavalry wavered.

Colonel Barclay could easily see from the organisation and

steadfastness of the Holkar cavalry that the command of the enemy army was in the hands of an officer more experienced and capable than the last of the Raghuvids. Barclay gave orders to outflank the right wing of the Indian army, then turn to the centre, and put the Indians under fire from both directions. If his plan succeeded, Holkar – cut off from Bhagavpur, his capital and main fortress – would be routed. This one single manoeuvre could bring an end to the war. The most important thing for Barclay was that no one should snatch the fruits of victory from him, or take the glory of leading such a fast-moving and well-led expedition.

Corcoran, meanwhile, was deep in thought. He saw that no one was in any condition, except for himself and possibly Sugriva, to command Holkar's troops.

The old Prince had never been a great warrior, even though he was brave. He lacked the coolness which some have naturally and others learn on the battlefield. Moreover, Holkar was troubled by the thought of the danger he'd allowed his daughter to fall into because of his imprudence. But he had great confidence in his friend Corcoran.

'Lord Holkar,' said the Breton, 'we've both made serious mistakes. Yours was to besiege that cursed temple with that scoundrel Robarts inside (may the heavens confound him!). And I was wrong to let you do it.'

'It was no fault of yours,' replied Holkar. 'I was the old fool who risked the liberty of my daughter for the pleasure of burning alive forty or fifty Englishmen.'

'Let's not speak of it,' interrupted the Breton, 'we should not speak of the past, think only of the future. Nothing is lost, if your horsemen hold firm. You, Lord Holkar, take command of the right wing, where you will face the sepoy cavalry, amongst whom Sugriva has some friends who may help us at the decisive moment. I will stay on the left, where I see Colonel Barclay has concentrated his forces and deployed his European regiment. Try not to let yourself be surrounded, and be bold. And don't be afraid or run away if you are outflanked. In any event, it should be safe to retreat in an orderly fashion.'

'And my daughter?' said the old man.

'She's getting on her elephant and will make her slow way back to Bhagavpur under the guard of Sugriva... And it is not a question of us defeating the English cavalry in battle, but of containment, and ensuring that we can get back to Bhagavpur intact. If we wait too long, Colonel Barclay's infantry will have time to get here, and we will be surrounded and cut to pieces. Tomorrow, with all our forces, we can fight a battle on equal terms, and then, on that day, we can talk of victory. Onwards, Holkar! When one has put oneself in danger by one's own mistakes, it is necessary to respond with a great show of daring. Sword in hand, by Jove! And remember your ancestor Rama who would have swallowed ten thousand Englishmen as if they were boiled eggs.'

Then, he turned towards the beautiful Sita, who was already mounted on her elephant.

'Sita,' said Corcoran, 'I will leave Louison with you. She understands her duties and how to fulfil them. Louison! Sita is your mistress, you owe her respect, love, fidelity and obedience... If you fail in that our friendship is over.'

But Sita's elephant did not want Louison's company. He

scowled at the tigress and tried to brush her away with his trunk. Louison, who was never patient, began to get irritated. Corcoran tried to calm her down.

'My dear,' he said, 'when your good qualities are as well known to the outside world as they are to me, then Scindia[33] (for that's the name of the elephant) will accord you a great welcome, but you must first get to know each other.'

Sita, who had a lot of influence over Scindia, her favourite elephant, forced him to make an alliance with the tigress, and the latter was able to join her in the howdah on the elephant's back. Louison lay at the feet of the Princess – happily, lazily curled up like an Angora cat. Every now and then Scindia turned his enormous head to look at Sita, and seemed jealous of the favours that she granted to Louison.

It was after making all these arrangements, and forcing Sita to leave with her escort, that Corcoran, free of all other cares, could turn his thoughts to covering the retreat of Holkar's army, because he did not wish to do battle today.

Time was pressing, and the English were about to charge. Barclay, having let his exhausted horses rest after their earlier exertions, gave the signal to attack.

The first wave of English cavalry was so determined that it broke through Corcoran's front line, and was about to attack the second line. But the Breton had positioned a cavalry squadron in ambush, hidden behind a small rise in the land. As the English cavalry were passing by, Corcoran charged with his squadron, causing disorder in enemy ranks. The Indians then rallied and rejoined the fighting, forcing the English back. Corcoran led by example, and spared nothing in his efforts.

While Barclay, astonished by this unexpected resistance, continued to urge on his soldiers.

In the midst of the battle, the two leaders met.

'Monsieur Corcoran,' said Barclay, 'so this is how you go about searching for the manuscript of the *Guru Karamta*. If I capture you, you will be shot. Mr Learned Man, indeed!'

'Colonel Barclay, if I capture you, you will be hanged!'

'Hanged? Me! A gentleman!' exclaimed the furious Barclay. 'Hanged!'

And he fired his revolver at Corcoran, lightly wounding him in the shoulder.

'Missed!' said Corcoran. 'This one will hit its target.'

And Corcoran returned fire, but the Colonel caused his horse to rear up, and it was the horse that received the bullet in its chest. Driven mad by pain, it carried its rider away from the battle.

The English squadrons slowly made their retreat. They were only gently pursued by Holkar's forces because Corcoran dreaded the arrival of Barclay's infantry.

But at the other end of the battlefield, it was going less well. The left wing of the English forces were led by the traitor Rao, who had joined the English army with Holkar's deserters. Holkar resisted valiantly, and even came close to defeating Rao, when unexpected reinforcements changed the balance of forces. The reinforcements were none other than John Robarts and his officers who, seeing the retreat of Corcoran and Holkar, had left the temple, remounted their horses and, guided by the sound of gunfire, thrown themselves into battle.

Soon Holkar's soldiers began to retreat, slowly at first, and then in disorder. Many of them gathered around Sita's elephant, which continued on its way to Bhagavpur. The fighting became more intense. The sepoys in the service of the East India Company, led by John Robarts, showed great determination. Holkar's horsemen, no longer certain of reaching Bhagavpur, fought back furiously.

But then Holkar was knocked off his horse by a sword-blow and fell at the feet of Scindia the elephant.

Sita gave a great cry of dismay.

The wise and serious Scindia gently picked up poor Holkar with his trunk – and placed the Prince on the palanquin next to his daughter. Then, realising the danger to his dear mistress, the elephant moved his enormous body against the flood of retreating and attacking soldiers. There were bursts of rifle fire all around, but the elephant, impassive as a god, brushed aside the enemy soldiers with his trunk, or trampled them underfoot – and received a hail of bullets without being troubled.

The sight of Louison, meanwhile, made the bravest soldier faint. The natural armour of Scindia and the powerful claws of the tiger provided a formidable defence for Holkar and Sita.

But in the end they had to retreat because of the enemy's superior numbers. Brave Sugriva, commanding the escort, had been thrown to the ground beneath his dying horse and was about to be taken prisoner. Holkar, grievously wounded, was unable to take command, and the Indians began to flee. While Corcoran, looking around him at the endangered right wing of Holkar's army, rode to its rescue, and in particular to the rescue of the unfortunate Sita.

Until then, Corcoran had only thought of trying to retreat in good order. But when he saw that Sita was once again close to falling into the hands of her kidnappers, he was overcome by fury. He gathered his best horsemen around him, and headed towards the wretched Rao, broke through the English cavalry and forced it into total retreat. With a thrust of his sword he knocked Rao to the ground, where he lay dying under the feet of many horses.

Then Corcoran went to rescue Sugriva – but John Robarts and the small number of Englishmen who were with him were retreating in the face of Corcoran's unstoppable charge. As they retreated, they led Sugriva away with his hands tied behind his back. Seeing this, Corcoran and some of his horsemen threw themselves on Robarts and his companions. The Breton was about to cut through Sugriva's ropes with his sword, but was astonished when Sugriva said to him in a low voice, 'What are you doing, Captain? Don't you see that I am planning to collect information? You will see me again in three or four days, and I hope I will have some good news.'

Corcoran scowled at John Robarts, who was returning at top speed to recapture his prisoner.

'By my faith,' said Corcoran to himself, 'this brave Indian makes war like I do, for the fun of it, and why stop him doing so? And what does it matter to me if Robarts is hanged or dies at the sword in battle? The difference is mere sophistry.'

As he was thinking this, he left Sugriva and caught up with the powerful Scindia, who was moving at a majestic and solemn pace – unhurried, as if he were marching on parade.

Louison walked alongside, less solemn no doubt, because she had a more capricious and joyful nature, but nevertheless proud to be contributing to the safety of the kingdom. Corcoran covered the retreat of Holkar's forces, and commanded the rearguard which was largely untroubled by the English forces.

He thrust his sword into Rao the traitor

Colonel Barclay feared a trap as he came closer to Bhagavpur, and for fear of being caught up in some ambush, he halted his army one league from Holkar's capital. He would need his infantry and artillery in order to embark on a proper siege. It wasn't only that the city was well defended. Its ramparts dated from the time when Holkar's ancestors, princes of the Maratha confederacy, stood up to the Tartar cavalry of Tamburlaine.[34] Since that time, deeper ditches had been dug, several breaches had been repaired and cannons placed on the old towers and walls.

So these were the circumstances in which Holkar resolved to defend Bhagavpur against the English. And Corcoran, full of confidence in his own ability and in the promises of Sugriva, dared to promise that the siege would not be successful. His first precaution was to bring his own ship, *The Son of the Tempest*, further up the Narmada, where he hid it in a bend of the river – so as to keep it out of the hands of the English, and so that he could, whenever he wanted, move from one bank of the river to the other.

16

How the brave Berar disliked the caresses of the cat-o'-nine-tails

On the day after the first battle, Colonel Barclay, now with his cannons and his infantry, tried to speed up the assault on Bhagavpur. His plan was to bring his artillery close to the walls of the fortress and use it to knock down one of the ramparts. The stones from the ramparts would then fall into the ditch – filling it up so that his soldiers could easily enter through the breach in the wall.

But he had not counted on the vigilance and the ability of Corcoran. In an artillery duel which lasted almost two hours, Corcoran managed to damage about twenty English cannons and set fire to some boxes of ammunition. The explosion that followed killed two or three hundred of Barclay's forces, English and sepoys, and the Colonel realised that a more traditional siege would be necessary.

He began digging a trench, but the sepoys were mediocre workmen – nimble but weak. The Europeans, enfeebled by the hot climate and already sick with fever, could do little work.

Moreover, they were discouraged by Corcoran's frequent sorties.

Corcoran, thanks to his ship, could come and go at will, moving from one bank of the Narmada to the other, deploying his twelve sailors and his first mate either on the ship or with the artillery on the ramparts.

Because of this auxiliary force, Corcoran was able to defy the English with impunity, harassing them with his cavalry. Several companies of Holkar's infantry on small boats were able to control the Narmada, in a way that began to make Colonel Barclay fear that he would have to lift the siege of Bhagavpur, for lack of food and ammunition.

But the courage and diligence of Corcoran could not overcome the discipline and unwavering steadfastness of the English. And after a siege that had already lasted fifteen days, the Captain – poorly supported by his Indian soldiers – was no longer in any doubt about the destiny of Bhagavpur and of Holkar. Already in the city, there were predictions of a final assault and a growing desire to surrender. If Corcoran hadn't been there, Holkar's soldiers would have been ready to rebel and hand the city over to Colonel Barclay.

One evening, when the English had finished their trenches and dug all the emplacements for their cannon, they began to fire with such force at the city gate closest to the river that the walls collapsed, and a large breach offered the attackers a way into the city.

Holkar, still suffering from his injury, asked Corcoran for advice. Sita was sitting close by.

'My friend,' said Holkar, 'it's all so desperate. The breach in the wall is more than fifteen paces wide, and there will be an assault tonight or tomorrow. What should we do?'

'By my faith,' replied Corcoran, 'I can see only three alternatives. First, you could surrender...'

Holkar looked horrified.

'I understand,' continued the Breton, 'that you do not want to be a prisoner of the English at any cost. Though, Lord Holkar, there are philanthropists in the East India Company who would be happy to grant you a pension that would assure you a tranquil old age – three or four thousand francs a year, for example...'

'I would rather die,' said Holkar.

'You are right to take that view, and that first alternative is worthless. The second option is for you to come on board my boat, *The Son of the Tempest*, with Sita, along with your diamonds and your gold and all that is most precious to you, and then go downriver to the sea under cover of night. Then, you could cross the Arabian Sea before the English had time to catch you, go through Egypt[35] and embark in Alexandria on the steamboat *Oxus*, whose captain, Antoine Kerhoël, is my friend, who does the crossing from there to Marseilles.'

'It's you who should leave with Sita,' interrupted Holkar. 'Captain, I entrust you with my daughter, who is dearer to me than anything else in the world. As for me, I will stay. The last of the Raghuvids should be buried beneath the ruins of his capital. I will die fighting, like Tippoo Sahib. I will not flee.'

'I agree,' exclaimed Corcoran, 'and that's what I was expecting you to say! Let's stay here a while and give these English scoundrels a proper welcome, so that not one of them returns to London to tell their tales to their countrymen. But don't worry, Sita will be taken to the boat in advance. Ali will accompany her. If there is some misfortune here, she will at least be safe.'

'Captain,' said Sita in a voice full of emotion, 'do you really think I wish to live without my father and…?'

She wanted to add, 'and without you'. But she pulled herself together and said, 'Either we die together, or we win together.'

'By Jove!' said the Captain, 'the English had better watch out.'

When they went outside to inspect the breach in the walls, a sepoy came up and asked to speak to them.

'Who are you?' asked the Breton. 'What is your name?'

'Berar.'

'Who sent you?'

'Sugriva.'

'Prove it.'

'This ring is my proof.'

'And what does Sugriva say?'

'He sent you this letter.'

Corcoran opened the letter and read:

Captain,

Berar – the friend who brings you this letter – can be trusted. He detests the English as much as you do.

At five o'clock in the morning, the assault will begin. I know because I overheard a conversation between Colonel Barclay and Lieutenant Robarts. Neither of them realised that I was listening. Some important news has come from Bengal. The sepoy garrison in Meerut has taken up arms and shot its European officers. From Meerut, the sepoys travelled to Delhi where they proclaimed the last Mughal Emperor as their leader. Five or six hundred English people were massacred.[36]

It is because of this news that Barclay has decided to risk all on the success of the assault on Bhagavpur tomorrow. The Governor of Bombay has ordered him to finish with Holkar and return. If tomorrow's assault fails, they will retreat.

For my part, I have not been inactive. I took the latest dispatches from Colonel Barclay's table, and five or six of my sepoy friends read them, and then spread the news throughout the camp. You will be able to judge the effect. I regret that I cannot be with you defending the breach – but I will be more useful to you in the English camp. Have high hopes and be prepared for everything.

Sugriva

An astonished Corcoran looked at the messenger.

'And how did you cross the English front-line?' he asked, somewhat mistrustfully.

'What does it matter, since I am here?'

'Why did you desert the English? Did they pay you badly?'

'On the contrary, they paid me very well.'

'You were not well fed?'

'I fed myself, buying my own rice so that the hands of the impure would not touch it.'

'Were you maltreated? Did you receive some kind of injury?'

He uncovered his lower back and showed Corcoran the enormous scars.

'Ah, I understand,' said Corcoran, 'these are the wounds of the cat-o'-nine-tails. You have been whipped?'

'Fifty times,' replied the sepoy. 'I fainted on the twenty-fifth and they continued to whip me. I was in hospital for three months, and I only left five weeks ago.'

'Who whipped you?' asked the Captain.

'It was Lieutenant Robarts… But we will deal with him, Sugriva and I, we won't leave him for a minute.'

'He's a well-guarded officer!' thought Corcoran.

And then he added out loud, 'What is Sugriva doing in the English camp? Is he free then?'

'Sugriva,' said the sepoy, 'slipped through their fingers. When he was taken prisoner, Robarts – who recognised him – wanted to keep him as a captive. But while the council of war was sitting, Sugriva spoke to a sepoy guard who was holding him in custody. The guard set him free and deserted with him. You can imagine the anger of the lieutenant. He wanted to shoot everybody, but Colonel Barclay calmed him down. Sugriva returned in the evening, disguised as a fakir, and made himself known to the sepoys. But none of them wanted to hand him over to the English, and if the English tried to take him the sepoys would rebel.'

'Excellent,' said Corcoran, who went to the palace to give the good news to Holkar, and then returned to the ramparts.

At he was returning, he saw in the darkness a shadow slip through the breach into the bottom of the ditch. It was Berar the sepoy returning to the English camp. Berar made a secret sign to the sepoy guard who was watching over the trenches, and entered the camp untroubled.

'I must say,' thought Corcoran, 'Colonel Barclay has some pretty unusual soldiers – and they fully deserve their pay.'

17

The final destiny of Lieutenant Robarts of the 21st Hussars

The night passed without incident. On both sides, they prepared for the following day's assault with rest and in total silence. The guards from each camp were so close to each other that they could easily have held a conversation. In appearance at least, all was quiet.

But in the area of the English camp occupied by the sepoys, one could hear instructions being given in a low voice, far from the ears of the European officers. Sugriva slipped in and out of the tents, passing on his mysterious orders.

Finally, the day began. A cannon shot signalled the start of the assault, and a first column of English soldiers, serving as the vanguard, with their bayonets fixed, clambered through the breach.

As they advanced, they were welcomed by gunfire from the front and the sides; five or six field guns firing grapeshot made a large hole in their ranks. A number of bombs, hidden at the bottom of the ditch by Corcoran, suddenly exploded beneath their feet. Half the column was destroyed in the blink of an eye. The others retreated rapidly from the breach and returned to their trenches.

Seeing this, Corcoran, who was commanding the battalion in charge of the breach, couldn't stop himself from laughing, and Holkar's soldiers, who had suffered almost no losses, seemed full of life and courage.

As for the Captain, standing at the breach, he was silent and smiling as if he had been attending a ball. He looked around, and without exaggerating the significance of the first success, awaited the second attack with confidence. Beside him stood old Holkar, full of enthusiasm. And behind them, Louison walked about with an air that was both serious and joyful, without scaring anyone, thanks to the precise and severe discipline that Corcoran had imposed on her. More than that, her intelligence, which enabled her to understand and foresee the desires of her master, inspired in Holkar's soldiers a superstitious respect for her.

They waited for a quarter of an hour.

'Have they already given up on the assault?' asked Holkar.

'No,' replied Corcoran, 'though I am troubled by this silence. Louison!'

On hearing his call, the tigress lifted an ear as if to understand more clearly the Captain's orders.

'Louison, my dear,' said Corcoran, 'we need some information. What is happening there in the trenches? You don't know? Well, go and find out... Go into their trenches, and grab as delicately as you can between your teeth the first Englishman that you find – an officer, if possible – and bring him to me delicately. But be especially cautious, swift and discreet.'

This entire discourse was accompanied by very precise gestures, and Louison lowered her head after each phrase to show that she had understood. She sped off like an arrow, crossed the breach with one leap, and went down into the ditch. With another leap she climbed the slope and a few seconds later she was inside one of the trenches, where the English, regrouped and reorganising, were preparing a second assault.

The first person whom Louison found within reach was a lieutenant of the 25th Line Infantry, the courageous James Stephens, of Cartridge-House, in the county of Durham. With one blow from her paw she knocked him over. And with one bite she seized him between her teeth and began to run back towards the breach.

Louison's action was so quick and so unexpected that the English had no time to respond. The tigress crossed the breach and deposited her prey at the feet of Corcoran, while looking at him in a manner that was both intelligent and warm, and which seemed to signify:

'Well, my dear master. Haven't I done my duty well?'

Unfortunately, Louison, who was a little too hurried and feared letting go of her prey, had squeezed the unfortunate gentleman too tightly, so that her teeth had entered his lungs, and by the time Lieutenant James Stephens of Cartridge-House was deposited on the ground in front of the Captain, he was dead.

'Poor lad!' said Corcoran. Louison, who had little knowledge of human anatomy, did not realise how tightly she was holding him. 'Anyway, let's try once more. Louison, my dear, you have committed a serious error. You have treated this Englishman as if he were a beefsteak cooked medium rare;

Lieutenant James Stephens was dead

you should have treated him as a gentleman and brought him here alive. So, try again – and be a bit more careful this time.'

The tigress understood perfectly Corcoran's words of reproach, and left, her head lowered, shamed at having failed in such a clumsy manner.

This time, the gentleman whom she brought back was so delicately clasped and so little damaged by her teeth and her claws that she would have been able to offer him entirely unwounded to Corcoran, if the English hadn't had the unfortunate idea of firing in the general direction of Louison. A bullet destined for the tigress entered two inches deep into the brain of the gentleman, which put an end to his life and his misfortunes – if he had any misfortunes, that is.

After this second attempt, Corcoran realised that it was going to be impossible to get precise information on the movements of the enemy in this way. But soon a great noise could be heard from another section of the ramparts where there were only a few guards. About one hundred and fifty or two hundred Englishmen had scaled the wall and entered the city. Already, Holkar's soldiers were throwing away their weapons and fleeing in the face of the enemy.

'Lord Holkar,' said Corcoran, 'stay here at the breach. I am going to where the English have got into the city. You must remain here – and if you allow them to force their way through, all will be lost, and we would have nothing more to do but perish.'

At the same time, he took with him a battalion from those who were guarding the breach, and marched towards the Englishmen who had scaled the wall.

First, Corcoran took the precaution of knocking over the ladders into the ditch so that no one could help the intruders. Then he barricaded the long road which they had entered, and which was, in fact, a cul-de-sac. Fortunately for him, the road was very narrow and he was able to complete this work in just a few seconds. Then he ordered his forces to attack the enemy from different directions, and he brought three field guns loaded with grapeshot and aimed them at the attackers. He called on the English to give themselves up.

The English tried to force a passage with their bayonets. Immediately, Corcoran opened fire. In the blink of an eye the road was filled with the dead and injured.

While he reloaded the field guns, Corcoran again called on the English to surrender. This time they did so. Only eighty of the Englishmen were still standing out of about two hundred who had entered Bhagavpur.

But Corcoran had no time to bask in his glory. A great tumult of cries and wailing made him fear there had been some catastrophe. He hurriedly returned to the breach and, on the way, encountered two or three hundred of Holkar's soldiers running away.

'Stop,' said Corcoran in a terrifying voice. 'Where are you running to?'

'Captain,' said one of the deserters, 'Holkar is mortally wounded. The English have crossed through the breach. Run for your life!'

'Run for your life, indeed!' exclaimed Corcoran. 'Miserable wretch, turn and face the enemy or I will blow your brains out, yours and all these cowardly scoundrels'.'

With that threat, the unfortunate Indian returned to the

breach, not feeling he had the courage to confront the Breton's anger. The others followed his example – it was more from fear than any other sentiment that they returned to face the enemy again.

However, the news was only too true. An enemy column of English soldiers and sepoys had resumed the assault, and even though Holkar had fought valiantly, the outcome of the day's fighting appeared to have been settled. Already, the victors had entered houses in the suburbs and begun to loot them.

Holkar, injured fifteen days earlier, had received a bullet in the chest and seemed close to death. Surrounded by a small group of faithful soldiers, he was lying on a carpet which they had hastily brought for him. An Indian surgeon was staunching the blood from his wound.

'Ah, my friend,' he exclaimed on seeing Corcoran. 'Bhagavpur is lost. Save my dear Sita.'

'Nothing is lost,' said Corcoran. 'You're alive, and best of all, you're winning! Take courage, Holkar, and the day will be ours.'

At these words, the Indians rallied around Corcoran. He closed the breach, broke the supply line between the English camp and the enemy column which had entered Bhagavpur, and sent his best troops in pursuit of the column – while guarding the breach himself and waiting for what would happen next.

His hopes were not misplaced. The intruders, seeing that they were so few in number, and in danger of being trapped in the city, feared that they would be taken prisoner. They retraced their steps and forced a passage through the ranks of the Indians, who did not stop them, and the English forces were able in this way to return to their trenches.

And at that moment, an unexpected event ensured Corcoran's victory.

Suddenly, thick smoke rose above the camp, behind the English lines. There was the sound of furious gunfire. The sepoys, led by Sugriva, had set fire to the tents, charged Colonel Barclay from behind, shot some English officers, spiked the cannons, set light to the ammunition boxes and thrown the camp into total chaos.

Corcoran decided this was the perfect moment. He put himself at the front of three of Holkar's regiments and advanced rapidly. On horseback, without uniform, dressed in white, as was his custom, and with his sword in his hand, he charged at the enemy.

Colonel Barclay was an old soldier who one could surprise but not fluster. He was not astonished by the treachery of the sepoys, and he gathered around him the two European regiments and began an orderly retreat. He took command of the cavalry himself and covered the rearguard. His haughty, furious countenance inspired respect and dread among the Indians.

Corcoran feared some new twist of fortune and did not want to push harder for victory. He was content to harass the English retreat for half an hour, and then return to Bhagavpur – making sure that the cavalry was keeping a close eye on the troop movements.

The dying Holkar was waiting for him. Next to the old man sat the beautiful Sita, on whose knees rested the head of her father.

'Is there no hope, dear Sita?' asked the Captain in a low voice.

Holkar was able to guess, rather than hear, the question.

'No, my dear friend,' he said. 'I am going to die. The last of the Raghuvids will be killed in battle, like all his ancestors, and I will not have had to see the entry of a triumphant enemy in the Palace of the Holkars. But my daughter, my daughter...'

'My father,' said Sita, 'don't worry about me. Brahma watches over all beings.'

'My friend,' continued the old man, 'I leave Sita to you. Only you can defend and protect her. Perhaps you alone would wish to do this. Be her husband, her protector and her father. She loves you, I know it, and you...'

Corcoran could only clasp the hand of the old man in silence, but his eyes said clearly enough to Sita that he loved her.

Holkar called over the most senior officers of his army.

'Here is my successor,' he said, 'my adopted son, and the husband of Sita. I leave him my kingdom, and I command that you obey him as you obeyed me.'

They all swore their allegiance. In just a few days, Corcoran, by his courage and generosity, had won over their hearts.

Towards the end of the day, Holkar died, having celebrated the marriage of his daughter according to the rites of Brahma. Corcoran was at the same time proclaimed Prince of the Marathas, and the following day he turned his attention to the pursuit of the English, leaving Holkar's daughter to fulfil her final duties towards her father.

Along the route that the English army had taken, Corcoran saw some unburied corpses. The sepoys, waiting in ambush in the jungle, had massacred the stragglers. Then, a short distance from the main route, Corcoran noticed from afar a strange object that resembled a hanged man.

Towards the end of the day, Holkar died

As he got closer, he saw that the hanged man was wearing a red uniform and epaulettes.

Closer still, he recognised the hanged man as Mr John Robarts, Lieutenant in Queen Victoria's Hussars.

He turned to Sugriva, who was on horseback next to him, and said, 'My dear Sugriva, destiny has taken away your prey. John Robarts has been hanged.'

Sugriva smiled with satisfaction.

'Do you know,' Sugriva asked, 'who hanged him?'

'You, perhaps?'

'Yes, Captain.'

'Hmmm,' said Corcoran, 'it would have been enough just to kill him. You are a little too vindictive, my dear friend.'

'Ah,' said the Indian, 'if only I had had more time to prolong his torture. But we were pressed for time, Berar and I. We followed him, step by step, through the night. There were five of us. Berar killed his horse with a rifle shot. Robarts fell to the ground and we were able to pick him up easily – he had a broken leg. He fired at us with his revolver, killing no one, but injuring one of our comrades. We tied his arms behind him, and Berar, having stripped his back, gave him fifty strokes of the whip, exactly the number which he had received on the orders of that gentleman.'

'What the devil!' said Corcoran, 'that's quite a memory you have. And what did he say, this gentleman as you call him?'

'Nothing. He rolled his eyes ferociously. One might have thought that he wanted to devour us all, but he didn't open his mouth.'

'And after that, what did you do with him?'

'When Berar had whipped him, it was my turn. With the

The tragic end of John Robarts, Lieutenant in the Queen's Hussars

help of my friend I put a rope round his neck, and I hanged him and then cut the rope three or four times, until he seemed to be dead. Finally, when he actually was dead, I returned to Bhagavpur.'

'By my faith,' said Corcoran who was something of a philosopher, 'it's written that "he who lives by the sword, dies by the sword". I feel sorry for poor Robarts, even though he was a bad sort. It's no thanks to him that I didn't get a bullet through my brains. Let's bury him decently, and say no more about it.'

18

How the dividends of the East India Company were reduced to nothing by the industry of Corcoran making several of its biggest shareholders groan

Colonel Barclay, still under pressure from the victorious Marathas, wanted to make sure his retreat didn't turn into a rout. He withdrew slowly, always facing the enemy, and found sanctuary in a fortress which belonged to his friend Rao, and which overlooked a stretch of the Narmada River. His little army was now reduced to three European regiments, because the sepoys had taken flight, or declared themselves on the side of Captain Corcoran. The Narmada, which bends like the Seine between the Pont de la Concorde and the suburb of Saint Denis,[37] looped round the fortress which was situated on a hill, and defended by lots of artillery pieces.

Just as Captain Corcoran was about to approach the fortress

and begin digging siege trenches, an English officer appeared with a white flag.

Sugriva, always keen for vengeance, said that he should be shot, and no quarter should be given to the enemy. But Corcoran had the Englishman brought before him.

The Englishman had an arrogant manner. He was the famous Captain Bangor, who had distinguished himself in the Sikh war,[38] and who had shot, in cold blood, after the victory, all his prisoners. In recognition of this glorious exploit, the East India Company promoted him and gave him twenty thousand rupees (about eighty thousand francs).

Corcoran received him with his customary politeness.

'Monsieur,' said the Englishman, 'Colonel Barclay has sent me to make peace.'

'Very good,' replied Corcoran. 'Peace is a beautiful thing, especially if the terms are right.'

'Monsieur, the terms are better than you could hope for,' said Bangor.

This made the Breton smile.

'Colonel Barclay,' continued Bangor, 'offers you your life and liberty, for you and your European companions (if you have any). And he won't even stop you from taking your luggage with you and a sum of money that does not exceed one hundred thousand rupees.'

'Oh, really?' said Corcoran. 'The Colonel is most kind, and has clearly thought through the details. Let me hear the rest of it.'

'As for the other terms,' said Bangor, 'first, the violations of human rights that you – a citizen of a friendly and neutral nation – have committed by making war against the East India

The Englishman had an arrogant manner

Company will be forgotten, and, second, you will provide us, when you depart, with the keys to Bhagavpur.'

'Is that all?' asked Corcoran.

'I missed out one of the principal conditions,' replied the Englishman. 'Colonel Barclay insists that you hand over the tame tigress whom you take everywhere with you, and who (once she has been stuffed) will be exhibited in the British Museum.'

On hearing these words, Corcoran turned to Louison, who was listening to the conversation in silence.

'Louison, my dear,' he said, 'did you hear what this *goddam* said? He wants to have you stuffed.'

The word 'stuffed' made Louison roar in such a manner that Bangor shivered to the marrow of his bones.

'So I imagine,' added Corcoran, 'you would want to shoot her first?'

The Englishman only had the strength to nod in affirmation. The word 'shoot' made Louison leap in the air as if she had just received three bullets in her heart. She looked at Bangor with a scowl that made him despair of ever eating beefsteak again, and made him fear that he would soon become beefsteak himself.

'Monsieur,' he said, with a troubled air, 'remember that I came here to parley with you under a white flag. It is a matter of human rights…'

'Human rights,' replied Corcoran, 'are not tigers' rights. And Louison, if you continue to irritate her with your British Museum and your mania for taxidermy, will ensure that in just three minutes your skeleton will end up in the Tigrish Museum.'

'England will avenge my death,' said Bangor haughtily, 'and Lord Palmerston…'[39]

'Bah! Louison cares as much for Palmerston as for an empty walnut. But to return to our business, go back to Colonel Barclay and tell him I am aware of his situation, and that any act of bravado is futile. I know for a fact that he doesn't have food for more than eight days, that his three European regiments have been reduced to seventeen hundred men, that my boat, *The Son of the Tempest*, armed with twenty-six large cannons, has closed off the Narmada, that you are in no position to come out of the fortress to attack us, and finally that if Colonel Barclay delays matters, he will be forced to surrender unconditionally, and I will not be able to answer for the life of any of my prisoners.'

'In that case Monsieur,' said Bangor confidingly, 'I am authorised to offer you one million rupees if you agree to leave with Holkar's daughter and abandon the Marathas to their fate.'

'And you,' said Corcoran, 'if you persist for one more moment in proposing such treason, I will have you impaled. Send my compliments to Colonel Barclay, and say to him that I will be beside the river in one hour's time should he wish to negotiate. After that time, there will be no more negotiations.'

Bangor had to content himself with this offer, and he left.

Barclay, who had only made such insolent propositions in order to disguise his predicament, softened when he learned that Corcoran knew everything about their situation. He accepted the request for a meeting with the victor, one hundred paces from the fortress.

'Colonel,' the Breton said to him, holding out a hand, 'you were wrong to get embroiled with me. You know that now, but it is never too late to make amends.'

'Ah, so you accept my conditions!' replied Barclay, joyfully. 'I was sure of it. In the end, what could you expect from that scoundrel Holkar, who would desert you at the first setback? A million rupees, moreover, is a lot of money – you wouldn't find that buried under any paving stones. So your fortune is made, and I can even, if you want, suggest a good investment for you with White, Brown and Company, in Calcutta. It's a solid business, which has made twenty million from cotton, and would give you 15 per cent on your money. That's where I intend to put my loot once we've taken Bhagavpur.'

'So that's what you're thinking,' said Corcoran, laughing. 'Well, my dear Colonel, you will have to think again. To be frank, I am offering you exactly what you offered me, that's to say, permission to leave with your weapons and your luggage. Additionally, you must recognise the independence of the kingdom of Holkar, and live in peace with his successor, the new king.'

'Holkar is dead?' exclaimed the astonished Barclay.

'Undoubtedly. You didn't know?'

'And who is his successor?'

'I am, Colonel. Since yesterday I have been known as Corcoran Sahib, or if you prefer, Lord Corcoran. My advancement has been rapid, hasn't it? And when I left Marseilles with Louison five months ago, I could hardly imagine that I would become King of the Marathas. But it is the Divine Will that I should make my fellow men happy, and that I should wear the crown. I will use, like someone else, the famous motto "Dieu et mon Droit".'[40]

'Let us speak from the heart,' said Barclay. 'You are French, you know about England and its power. You do not think, like most of these darkies, that Brahma and Vishnu are going to appear from the Empyrean Heaven[41] to throw the English into the sea. You know perfectly well that behind the seventeen hundred European soldiers that are with me here is the all-powerful East India Company, with its headquarters in London, and which can send to Calcutta, if needed, one hundred, two hundred, three hundred, six hundred thousand men. However courageous you are (and I recognise that I have never met such an intrepid adversary) you are certain to perish. So instead, don't perish. Be the king, if that's what you want. Reign, govern, administer and legislate: we will do you no harm. More than that: we will help you. I can commit to that in the name of the East India Company. Your enemies will be our enemies, and our soldiers will be at your service.'

'Many thanks,' replied Corcoran, 'but I fear no one, and I have no use for your soldiers.'

'Think about it. One always has need of someone, and especially the East India Company.'

Corcoran kept silent for a few moments.

'And what is the price,' he said eventually, 'of your offer of an alliance? Because you will do nothing for nothing.'

'There are only two conditions,' said the Englishman. 'The first is that you pay twenty million rupees each year to...'

'My friend,' interrupted Corcoran, 'you have a great weakness. You only ever talk about money. I knew a bailiff in Saint-Malo who is like you in the way that one drop of water resembles another. He is tall, thin, dry, sad and hard, and he only speaks to people in order to get them to empty their wallets.'

'Monsieur,' responded Barclay with the dignity of one who

has been offended, 'the bailiff of whom you speak doesn't have the might of England behind him.'

'By Jove, if all of England is behind you, then all of France is behind the bailiff, especially the police who function as his halo. Once, I heard him at the courts shouting "Silence" with a voice so strong and so imposing that you would at first glance have mistaken him for the Emperor Charlemagne.'

'Monsieur,' said Barclay impatiently, 'let's not bother ourselves with these stories of Saint-Malo, bailiffs and the Emperor Charlemagne. Will you, yes or no, pay an annual tribute of twenty million rupees to the East India Company?'

'If I pay up,' replied Corcoran, 'who will reimburse me? All my savings and possessions, apart from my ship, can be held in the palm of my hand.'

'Why are you speaking of your current possessions? Just double or triple taxes. It's your subjects who will pay.'

'But what if they revolt? If they refuse to pay?'

'Well, we will come to your rescue.'

'I need to think about this.'

In fact, he had already thought about it, or rather he had no need to think about it, but he wanted to see what else was in the Englishman's bag.

'What is the second condition?' he continued.

The Colonel appeared at first to hesitate a little, then he said casually, 'Listen, dear Monsieur. I trust you, yes, I trust you totally, I promise you. But it is not only up to me. So, the Company wants its guarantees. For example, an English officer who lives close to you, who could be your friend, who...'

'...who would watch over all my activities, and who would inform the Governor-General about them. That's right, isn't it?' said Corcoran with a smile. 'This friend would watch for the right moment to wring my neck, as you did for Holkar. You call that a friend, I call that a spy…'

'Monsieur!' exclaimed Barclay.

'Now don't get angry. I'm really just a sailor, and a man who was poorly educated. I call things by their names. And two words are as good as a hundred. So I want nothing from you and the East India Company. I will keep my rupees, you keep your spy… or rather your friend.'

'Monsieur,' said Barclay, 'there is still time to talk. You're dazzled by your first success, but surely you cannot hope to resist the English all on your own. It's best to make peace, believe me.'

He was still speaking when Holkar's cavalrymen brought over a messenger who was carrying a letter intended for the English camp. Corcoran broke the seal and read out loud the following message.

> *Lord Henry Braddock, Governor-General of Hindustan to Colonel Barclay*
>
> Colonel Barclay is advised that the Sepoy Revolt is about to gain control of the Kingdom of Oudh. Lucknow has proclaimed the last King's son, a boy of ten years old, as ruler. His mother is regent. Sir Henry Lawrence is under siege in the fortress. Almost the entire Ganges valley is on fire. Peace must be made with Holkar, no matter what the cost, and you must go to the aid of Sir Henry Lawrence. Any delay, and old scores will be settled.[42]
>
> Signed
> Lord Henry Braddock

Barclay looked dismayed. He held out his hand to take the letter.

'Take it,' said Corcoran. 'You know better than me, without doubt, the signature of Lord Henry Braddock.'

The Colonel looked at the piece of paper for a long time. He was less concerned with his own fate than with that of his compatriots. He was witnessing the collapse of the English empire in India in just a few days because of the sepoys' efforts, and he was despondent that he could not come up with an easy remedy. After a long silence, he turned to Corcoran and said:

'I no longer have anything to hide. Let peace be agreed if that is what you want. I would ask you not to trouble our retreat.'

'Agreed.'

'As for the expenses of war…'

'You will pay them,' Corcoran interrupted him brusquely. 'I know it is hard to spend one's money when one thought one was going to take away someone else's. But you can get away with it by reducing the dividends of the shareholders of the most-exalted, most-powerful and most-glorious East India Company, or if it is too painful to reduce the dividend, you can redistribute part of the capital. That's a very common practice among several of the most illustrious companies in France and England.'

'You have the upper hand,' said Barclay, 'so your wishes prevail over mine. Will it be necessary to add to the agreement that the East India Company recognises Holkar's successor?'

'As you please, but it is hardly something that I care about. If I am the strongest, I know that the English will be my friend until death, but should my fortunes change they will try to hang

The victorious Corcoran

me, to avenge themselves for the fright I gave them. So let's leave aside these diplomatic lies and live as good neighbours if we can.'

'By the heavens,' exclaimed the Englishman, 'you are right! I think you must be the most loyal and the most sensible gentleman I have ever met, and I am proud, yes, in truth, I am proud and fortunate to shake your hand. Goodbye then, Lord Corcoran, since for now you are the legitimate king. Until we meet again!'

'May God guide you, Colonel,' said the man from Saint-Malo, 'and never return unless it is as a friend. Louison, my dear, give your paw to the Colonel.'

Early that same evening, the treaty was written and signed. The following day, the English began their march towards Oudh, followed as far as the frontier by Corcoran's cavalry.

19

An interesting philosophical conversation on the duties of the Maratha royalty. Holkar's funeral oration.

Fifteen days after the departure of the English, Corcoran returned to his capital. With the beautiful Sita, he quietly enjoyed the fruits of his prudence and courage. Holkar's entire army was eager to recognise him as the legitimate sovereign, and the *zamindars* (district governors)[43] obeyed, without any apparent reluctance, the son-in-law and successor of the last of the Raghuvids.

'Well,' he said one morning to Sugriva, whom he had made his Prime Minister, 'this is not all just about ruling. My reign should serve a purpose, because in the end kings haven't been put on earth simply to eat breakfast, lunch, dinner and have a good time. What do you think, Sugriva?'

'My Lord,' replied Sugriva, 'that wasn't part of the original plan of Brahma and Vishnu when they created the earliest kings.'

'But first, do you really think the kings are descended directly from these two mighty gods?'

'My Lord,' replied the Brahmin, 'nothing is more likely. Brahma, who created every being – including lions, jackals, toads, monkeys, crocodiles, mosquitoes, vipers, boa constrictors, camels with two humps, bubonic plague and deadly cholera – could hardly have left kings off this particular list.'

'It seems to me, Sugriva, that you don't have much respect for this noble and glorious segment of the human species.'

'My Lord,' replied the Brahmin, who lifted his hand to form the shape of a cup, 'didn't you make me promise always to tell the truth?'

'That's correct.'

'If you would prefer that I lie, nothing would be easier.'

'No, no, that's not necessary. But you would agree at least that not all kings are as disagreeable and as harmful as the plague or as cholera.'

Sugriva began to laugh silently in the Indian manner, and showed two rows of white teeth.

'Let's see,' continued Corcoran, 'with what could you reproach Holkar? Wasn't he of noble birth? Sita assures me that he was the direct descendant of Rama, son of Dasharatha, and the most intrepid of men.'

'Certainly.'

'Wasn't he brave?'

'As brave as the bravest soldier.'

'Wasn't he generous?'

'Yes, to those who flattered him. But half of his people

were dying of hunger outside the doors of the palace. He did nothing for those poor devils except say, "God will help you".'

'At least you will tell me that he was just.'

'Yes, but only when he had no desire to take away someone else's property. I myself saw him cut off people's heads after dinner for his own pleasure and to improve his digestion.'[44]

'They must have been the heads of scoundrels, who deserved decapitation.'

'Probably. At least I hope they weren't honest people whose faces displeased him. And look, what do you really know about old Holkar? How much money did he leave when he died?'

'Eighty million rupees,[45] that's apart from his diamonds and other precious stones.'

'And, honestly, do you think that any self-respecting king should be so rich?'

'Maybe he was thrifty,' said Corcoran.

'Thrifty! You know better than that!' Sugriva replied bitterly. 'For forty years he spent billions of rupees to satisfy the most foolish fantasies that can enter the spirit of a worshipper of Brahma. He built palaces by the dozen – a summer palace, a winter palace, a palace for every season. He diverted rivers so that he could have fountains in his gardens; he bought the most beautiful diamonds in India to decorate the hilt of his sword, and owned swords by the hundred. He brought slaves from each of the five continents. He fed and housed thousands of buffoons and parasites, but would impale anyone who tried to tell him the truth.'

'But then where did he get all that money?'

'From everyone here. That's to say from the pockets of poor people, and from time to time he would cut off the head of a *zamindar* in order to take control of his estate. And that's the only popular thing he ever did, because the people hate the *zamindars* more than death.'

'Really?' said Corcoran. 'That same Holkar, whom I thought, because of his white beard and his gentle, venerable manner, was a virtuous patriarch – a present-day Rama or Dasharatha. Was he really the scoundrel you describe? For God's sake, then, who can we believe in?'

'No one,' said the Brahmin pithily, 'because there is only one man in a hundred who would not be ready to commit crimes if he had absolute power. It may not happen on the first day, nor even on the second or the third, but everyone slides down that slope, without noticing. Do you know the history of the famous Aurangzeb?'

'Probably, but tell me anyway.'

'Well, he was the fourth son[46] of the Great Mughal who ruled in Delhi. Because he was pious, virtuous and had wisdom that had been well tested, his father favoured him ahead of his brothers, and named him as his successor. Once Aurangzeb was in a position of power, his piety melted like lead in a furnace, his virtue rusted like iron in water and his wisdom ran away like a gazelle pursued by hunters. His first act was to lock up his father. His second: to cut off the head of his brothers; the third: to have their friends and allies impaled. Even though his father was in prison and could no longer cause him any trouble he poisoned him. And do not believe that Brahma or Vishnu struck him down, or even opposed his plans. He died at the age of eighty-eight having accumulated wealth, victories and riches of every kind, honoured as a god, and without suffering even once from a stomach ache.'

'By Jove,' said Corcoran, 'I must admit that if all the princes of your country resemble poor Holkar or the illustrious Aurangzeb, then you are clearly wrong to mourn their death and therefore wrong to fight against the English who are getting rid of them for you.'

'I don't agree,' replied Sugriva, 'because the English lie, cheat, betray, oppress, pillage and kill just as much as our own princes, and there's no way of escaping them. Suppose that Colonel Barclay succeeded Holkar, it would be ten times worse, because he would take our money just like his predecessor, and, what's more, we would have nothing to gain by assassinating him. If he was killed, they would just send a second Barclay from Calcutta, just as ferocious and greedy as the first. Holkar, however, always feared having his throat cut, and sometimes that fear taught him good sense and moderation. And, in the end, he knows that a high-caste Brahmin like me is born an equal of kings, and he should be careful about insulting us. Whilst the brutal English (I've seen them in Benares) strike us Brahmins with whips to make us take our place with the masses. They enter our buildings in their boots, defiling everything as they go, without any fear of the consequences, even in the holy temple of Jagannath,[47] where the great hero Rama would not have entered without having performed the seven penitences and the seventy purifications.'

During this discourse, Corcoran was thinking deeply.

'It would have been best,' he thought, 'to marry Sita and then without delay search for the famous *Guru Karamta*, rather than accept without reflection Holkar's kingdom. But the wine has been opened, so it's best to drink it. I would have to be very ill-fated not to be a more honest man than my predecessor or than the glorious Aurangzeb. Moreover, I realised, when Barclay departed, that the spiteful English, who blame me for having forced them out of Bhagavpur, will sooner or later take their revenge on me and return with an army. I am a good sport, and will be ready and waiting. We shall see then who is the winner.'

Then he turned to Sugriva.

'My friend,' he said, 'Louison and I, we are the kind of people who are scared of nothing, and if apart from the Holkar kingdom, we were offered China, Indochina, the Malacca[48] peninsula, and all of Afghanistan to govern, we wouldn't be terribly troubled. I will show you from tomorrow that the job of being a king isn't so difficult.'

'My Lord,' exclaimed Sugriva while joining his hands in the shape of a cup above his head. 'Lord Corcoran, most knowledgeable of heroes, with your bright and shining countenance, with your eyes more beautiful than the flower of the blue lotus, let Brahma give you the good fortune of Aurangzeb and the wisdom of the sons of Dasharatha.'

20

What happened next

Two days later, the following proclamation was displayed on every street in Bhagavpur and in all the towns of the kingdom:

From King Corcoran to the noble, powerful, invincible Maratha nation:

It has pleased the immortal, incorruptible and righteous Eternal Being to take from us the glorious Holkar after he had chased away the red-coated barbarians who came from England to kill the faithful followers of Brahma, to take their treasure and to put their women and children into slavery.

Equally, it pleased the glorious Holkar to adopt me as his son, and to give me his own daughter to be my wife, my much-loved Sita, the last descendant of the noble Rama, who defeated Ravana and the demons of the night.

My plan is to make myself worthy of this honour by governing the kingdom according to the sacred law of the Vedas and the counsel of wise Brahmins, to leave no crime unpunished, and to protect the weak, especially widows and orphans.

Corcoran's proclamation

After this preamble, Corcoran called first for all the *zamindars* in the kingdom to come to Bhagavpur. Then he invited all the Marathas to elect three hundred deputies (one for every fifty thousand inhabitants) who would make the laws, scrutinise public expenditure, point out any abuses and decide on the remedy. Corcoran Sahib (Lord Corcoran) would only be charged with the execution of the laws. All men aged twenty and above would be electors, and would be eligible as candidates.

This last point displeased Sugriva.

'What?' he said. 'So an impure Pariah could be seated next to a Brahmin!'

'Why not?'

'But if he touches me I will have to purify myself by bathing in the sacred waters of the Narmada.'

'So what, have a bath then. You can never take too many baths.'

'But…'

'Would you like to be touched by an Englishman?'

Sugriva made a gesture which indicated repugnance and horror.

'You may have to choose between these two defilements.'

'My Lord,' responded Sugriva, 'believe me, do not insist on this. You will see that it will work out badly for you. You will be deserted as quickly as you were rallied to, and Colonel Barclay will return and take your place.'

'My friend,' said the Breton, 'I am not a legitimate king. My father was neither a son of Raghu nor of a Great Mughal. He was a fisherman from Saint-Malo. In truth, he was stronger, braver and better than all the kings I've known, or of whom history has spoken, and he was a French citizen. He was, in my eyes, superior to everyone; but in the end he was only a man. And he too had the sentiments of a man, that's to say he loved his fellow men, and he never did anything evil or contemptible. That's the only inheritance I received from him, and I want to keep it until the day I die.

'Good luck has provided me with the opportunity to give Holkar and all of you a hand in defeating the English – and that is perhaps my natural vocation. And the same good luck has given me my wife, my dear Sita, the most beautiful and also the best of all of the daughters of mankind – and as a result of which I became a powerful monarch fifteen days ago. But in spite of the example of the famous Aurangzeb which you quoted to me yesterday, my new-found regal status has not turned my mind. I would have just as much pleasure wandering the world in my ship, knowing no master but myself, as governing the entire Maratha Empire. If I agree to carry the sceptre, it's on condition of providing justice as much to Pariahs as to Brahmins, as much to peasants as to *zamindars*. If anyone wants to prevent me doing this I will take off my crown and put it in a corner, and then I will depart with Sita, whom I love more than the sun, the moon and the stars. After that you can organise matters with Barclay as you wish. Should you then destroy and impale each other, that's your business. I love human beings enough to devote myself to helping them, but not – if they don't want help – in spite of them.'

'The more I listen to you,' said Sugriva, 'the more I think you are the eleventh incarnation of Vishnu, because your words are so full of good sense and reason.'

'If I was the god Vishnu,' replied the Breton, laughing,

'you would have to obey me. So now you must distribute my proclamation and prepare a huge room for the representatives of the Maratha people, because I would like my parliament to open in exactly three weeks' time.'

Louison, who was listening to this conversation, smiled. She expected to have her place at the right of the thrones on which Corcoran Sahib and Sita would be seated. Perhaps she would also be able to sniff out the new and terrible dangers that her friend was about to encounter.

21

About the new friend whom Corcoran provided to the wise Brahmin Lakmana, and about the duties of friendship

But it wasn't all over. Most of the *zamindars* pledged obedience to their new master unwillingly. Several of them had aspired to the hand of Sita and the estates of Holkar. They all wished to remain independent, each in their own province, where they could perpetuate the tyranny of the 'good times' under the old king. However, no one dared take up arms against Corcoran. He was feared and respected. Many people considered him, as Sugriva had said, to be the eleventh incarnation of Vishnu. And Louison, whose powerful claws had accomplished so many marvellous exploits, was seen as the terrifying Kali, goddess of war and carnage. They were terrified of even catching her eye. People fell to the ground, their hands shaped like cups, as she passed through the streets of Bhagavpur, and she was accorded an almost divine status.

One man alone believed this was the favourable moment to grab the throne and commit an act of treason by killing Corcoran. He was one of the principal Maratha *zamindars*, a Brahmin of high birth, named Lakmana, who was thought to have descended from the younger brother of Rama and thereby have a claim to Holkar's kingdom. Even during the rule of Holkar, he'd tried several times to make himself independent, and entered into intrigues with Colonel Barclay. But after the defeat of the English he was the first to hurry to the side of Corcoran Sahib, to prostrate himself in front of the new king and declare his devotion.

In fact, he was waiting for a favourable occasion to reveal his true purpose – treason – and to stir up rebellion among the people. He invited all of those who were discontented to his house. He complained that the sacred law of Brahma had been violated by handing Holkar's crown to a European adventurer. He preached in favour of the return of old customs. He accused Corcoran of wearing boots made of cow leather (which was true and was an act of terrible sacrilege in the eyes of the Marathas). And, finally, Lakmana armed his fortresses, placed artillery guns on the ramparts and brought in supplies of gunpowder and cannonballs.

Sugriva knew about this and wanted Lakmana's head to be cut off before he could become dangerous, but Corcoran refused.

'My Lord,' said the faithful Brahmin, 'this is not how your glorious predecessor Holkar would have acted. At the slightest suspicion, he would have given the traitor a hundred strokes with a stick on the soles of his feet.'

'My friend,' said the Breton, 'Holkar had his methods,

which did not prevent him, as you know, from being betrayed and from dying. And I have my own methods. It's for Brahma to prevent such crimes. Only he can be sure of the facts, and would not therefore risk condemning an innocent man. But no man should be punished for a crime until after he has committed it. Without such a rule, there would be terrible mistakes and frightful remorse.'

'At least this Lakmana should be kept under surveillance,' said Sugriva.

'By whom? Me? I would have to create a police force, take into my service the most infamous scoundrels in the country, worry myself with a thousand details, always fearing treason. I would have to spy on and follow this man who is perhaps not planning anything. I would poison my own life with mistrust and suspicion.'

'But my Lord,' said Sita, who was listening to this discussion, 'imagine that at any moment Lakmana might assassinate you. You should be on guard, and if not for you, my dear Lord, whose eyes have the colour and the beauty of the blue lotus, then do so at least for me, who prefers you as you are, here on earth, rather than in heaven, in the resplendent palaces of the sublime Indra, father of gods and man.'

As she spoke, her eyes filled with tears, and she threw herself into the arms of Corcoran. He held her tenderly to his chest, looked at her for a moment and said, 'If that's what you want, my Sita, you sweet and charming creature to whom I can refuse nothing. If that's what you want, what both of you want, well, I agree then, and I will place the dreadful Lakmana under surveillance in such a way that will make him forever curse the day he formed his plan to take away my crown. Louison! Come here, Louison!'

The tigress came to Corcoran affectionately and gently rubbed her beautiful head against his knees. Her eyes looked attentively at the eyes of her friend and tried to work out what he was thinking.

'Louison, my dear,' he said, 'pay attention to what I am about to tell you. I need you to use all your powers of understanding.'

The tigress wagged her powerful tail and paid extra attention.

'There is in Bhagavpur,' continued the Breton, 'a man whom I suspect of having evil designs. If he's doing what I think he is, that's to say that he's planning an act of treason, I want you to tell me.'

Louison turned successively in each of the four directions of the compass, sniffing out the traitor with her pink nose, trimmed with thick whiskers, and offered to bring him to justice.

'So that there can be no mistake, I am going to call him here… Sugriva, go and find Lakmana and bring him here willingly or by force.'

Sugriva hurried off with this message and reappeared soon afterwards, followed by the seditious Brahmin. He was a man of average height, whose fiery, deep-set eyes were full of stifled hate. His prominent cheekbones, and his ears that stuck out like those of a Tartar and other such carnivores, seemed to declare him a master of artifice and destruction.

He did not seem surprised that he had been summoned, and from his first words, he swore that he had always regarded

Corcoran as his true lord and master. He responded to the incriminating evidence of Sugriva with a sermon on fidelity which did not persuade the Breton. His mistrust redoubled when Sugriva, who had secretly got his hands on the Brahmin's papers, suddenly and theatrically produced them. They were proof of a shadowy conspiracy, in which Lakmana was the chief conspirator. The plan was to assassinate Corcoran during the festival of the Goddess Kali.

The Brahmin was stupefied. All his intrigues had been uncovered. He was defenceless in the hands of his enemy, and he now awaited only death. But he didn't know about the generosity of the Breton.

'I could have hanged you,' said Corcoran, 'and even though I despise you, I will let you live. Moreover, however guilty you may be, you had neither the time nor the ability to carry out your crime – and that's enough to make me spare your life. I will not even do you any harm. I will not take your palace, or your rupees, or your cannons, or your slaves. I will not lock you up, I will not make it impossible for you to do harm. I will let you run about, conspire, scream, curse, slander, insult – that's your right. But if you take up arms against me, if you try to kill me, you are a dead man. From today I am providing you with a new friend who will never leave your side and who will inform me of all your plans. This friend is discreet, because she cannot speak. She is incorruptible because she has such frugal tastes, and, apart from sugar, there is nothing – unlike others in the world – that she likes enough to seduce her. As for being scared, that's impossible. Her courage and devotion are greater that anyone's. In short – it's Louison!'

On hearing these words, Lakmana became pale with terror, and all his limbs trembled.

'Lord Corcoran,' he said, 'have pity on me. I…'

'You have nothing to fear,' said the Breton. 'If you are loyal to me, Louison will be your friend. If you conspire against me, Louison, who knows everything, will soon tell me, or better still, with just one scratch from her claws put an end to the conspiracy and the chief conspirator… Louison, my beautiful, give Sugriva a proof of your wisdom. What is the finest jewel in this world?'

Louison lay down at the feet of Sita, and looked at her tenderly.

'Well done,' responded Corcoran. 'And now look at that Brahmin. Is he a man one can trust? Yes or no?'

The tigress slowly approached Lakmana, and sniffed him with an air of mistrust and then looked at Corcoran with her doubting eyes.

'You see, Sugriva,' said the Breton, 'she is telling me that she has smelled the odour of a scoundrel, and that she feels quite queasy. Louison, my dear, look at this man. Follow him, escort him, watch him, and if he commits an act of treachery, you should take him by the throat.'

With these words he sent Lakmana away, and he, quite terrified, left the palace. Louison walked behind him with admirable seriousness. One could see that she had been charged with overseeing the security of the state.

22

How Louison fell victim to treachery. A dreadful catastrophe

The contemptuous generosity of Corcoran did not touch the hardened heart of Lakmana. He continued to conspire in the shadows, but he dropped his original plan to attempt an armed revolt in the streets of Bhagavpur. The companionship of Louison, from which he could rarely escape, prevented him from plotting easily with his fellow conspirators. He almost believed that the tigress had, by special command of Brahma, the power to read his heart and know all his thoughts.

In spite of this, he had five or six barrels of gunpowder brought into his house, which he claimed were filled with wine. Louison, even though she was very curious, did not realise what he was plotting, and Sugriva himself believed that the Brahmin was happily filling his wine cellar. He even joked about it several times with Lakmana who, without showing any emotion, promised to let him taste a little of this exquisite wine after a few days. 'It is,' Lakmana said, 'Château Margaux of the highest quality.'

While he pretended to be merry and think only of feasts, Lakmana was secretly preparing to cause a catastrophe. He had cleared out an old tunnel, one hundred paces long, which led, by various detours known only to him, to an abandoned wine cellar in Holkar's palace. It was in that cellar, situated beneath the large hall where the first meeting of the Maratha parliament was supposed to take place, that Lakmana had got his two loyal servants to put the six barrels of gunpowder. And it was Lakmana himself, during one of Louison's brief absences to visit Corcoran in the palace, who put in place the fatal fuse that was destined to set light to the gunpowder and blow up, along with Corcoran and Sita, all the most powerful lords of the Maratha lands, and all those who might be claimants for the throne.

Louison, spirited and curious as she was, knew nothing of this stratagem. For three-quarters of each day, she carried out her duties conscientiously, following the Brahmin's every step, and watching him with a suspicious eye. He, on the contrary, always gentle and affectionate, attempted to win her over. He thought at first of poisoning her, but Louison refused all his offerings. This was because Corcoran had forbidden her to eat food from outside, which irritated the tigress a bit. Her sole defect was her gluttony. No one is perfect.

Lakmana, seeing that she was on her guard, tried to take her outside Bhagavpur in the hope that the sight of the great forests would tempt Louison, and that she would want to regain her freedom by returning to the wild. Louison followed him out of the city with pleasure, but as much as she wanted to be in the jungles and the mountains, she always returned to wherever they were staying.

He wanted to get rid of her at all costs. One morning, he led her to the fortress of Ayodhya, ten leagues away from Bhagavpur, which was part of Lakmana's territory and where the garrison would obey only him. At the top of the main tower, which oversaw the Narmada Valley, and from where one could see the blue mountains of the Ghats, was a room whose entire floor, except for one narrow part of it, was an enormous trapdoor. It was from here that the Brahmin threw his enemies into dungeons more than sixty feet below.

Lakmana, followed closely as always by Louison, opened the door to the room. The tigress, who was curious like all women and most cats, and who was disheartened by the dark staircase which she had just climbed in the footsteps of the Brahmin, saw an open window from where she would be able to see the wonderful countryside, without equal in the universe. She forgot her customary prudence and ran headlong into the room. Alas, this was just what the treacherous Lakmana was expecting.

The trapdoor, whose catch he had just released, opened suddenly beneath the weight of our poor friend, who fell into a terrifying chasm, and was unable to cling on to anything as she plunged downward. She barely had time to let out a cry or a roar or invoke the gods of divine justice against the perfidious Brahmin. Her fall caused a dull thud, like that of a bunch of grapes being crushed against a wall. Lakmana looked down into the opening, listened for a moment, heard nothing, and let out, even though he was alone, a loud burst of laughter, which would have made even his close cousin, Lucifer, shiver in the depths of hell.

Then he closed the door, went down the staircase, climbed

Our poor friend fell into a terrifying chasm

into his palanquin, and escorted by several servants, pretended to head towards Bombay. It would be presumed that he would be going to Bombay to seek asylum with the English, but in fact he secretly left his palanquin at nightfall and returned to his house in Bhagavpur without anyone seeing him.

Everything was ready. He had caused the death of the only witness whose testimony and claws he feared, and the day of the crime approached. Corcoran, busy with other cares and thinking Lakmana had left for Bombay, congratulated himself on his flight because it meant he didn't have to punish a conspirator. But there was a bitter feeling mixed with this satisfaction.

He was astonished not to see the return of Louison, otherwise so reliable, especially at dinner time. He feared that she had not been able to resist the attraction of liberty and life in the wild. He accused her of ingratitude. Alas! Poor Louison. He did not know that she had fallen victim to an infamous act of treason. Even less did he know the whereabouts of her cowardly killer.

Finally, the day arrived that had been fixed for the meeting of the representatives of the Maratha people. Enormous crowds filled the streets and squares of Bhagavpur. Six hundred thousand Indians had come from a thirty-league radius to bless the name of Corcoran Sahib and the beautiful Sita, the last descendant of the Raghuvids.

The two of them, mounted on the back of Scindia the elephant, both dressed in clothes of gold and silver, adorned with diamonds and precious stones of unimaginable value, advanced majestically through the bowing crowds, who admired the beauty, strength and genius of Corcoran and the

He set light to the fuse

incomparably gentle beauty of Sita. Then they both, followed by all the elected representatives of the people, paid homage in the great temple of Bhagavpur to the resplendent Indra, the Being of all Beings, father of the gods and of mankind. They all returned with great pomp to the palace where Corcoran sat on his throne, with Holkar's daughter at his side and the assembly facing him.

Lakmana, hidden behind the shutters of his house, saw the cortège pass by and it made him shake with rage. The fuse which would ignite the gunpowder and blow up the king and the entire parliament was already in place. It was only a matter of setting light to it, and it would then burn for seven hundred seconds, so that Lakmana would not be buried by his own crime. Beside him was his only accomplice, a wretched servant, who hadn't dared refuse his support to the horrifying crime, for fear of being stabbed by his treacherous master.

The Brahmin waited another quarter of an hour, so that the entire assembly had time to gather in the palace. Then, slowly, without remorse, he lit the fuse.

23

The conclusion of this admirable story

While the assassin was making his final preparations, Corcoran stood up in a majestic manner and said:

'Representatives of the glorious Maratha nation

'The reason I have gathered you all here today, contrary to the custom of preceding kings, is to put into your hands the power that the dying Holkar invested in me by right of adoption.

'I have no desire for the throne. I only wish to sit on it with your consent. I do not wish to rule because I have the power to do so, but because you have freely elected me.'

(All the people cried out: 'Corcoran Sahib forever! May he reign over us and our children.')

He continued:

'All men are born equal and free; but because they are not all as strong as each other, it is necessary to intervene sometimes to protect the weak and ensure that the law is respected. That is the duty with which you are charging me. You should make laws which are just and which respect the right to liberty.

'My predecessors forcibly conscripted an army of two hundred thousand soldiers. I will not copy them. I will keep an army of only ten thousand soldiers – all volunteers. That will be enough to maintain law and order. But I will provide weapons to everyone so that they can defend their liberty against the English, should they return, or against me if I abuse my authority.

'The total amount of taxation this year will be one hundred million rupees. You will see for yourselves next year what it will be reduced to. And I will myself pay, out of Holkar's private treasury, the cost of public services for this year. This will be my present for the joyous future of the Maratha people. I've calculated it all. Thirty millions rupees should be enough and more for the needs of the state.'

With these words, everyone cried out in admiration. The representatives wept out of affection. Never before, in any country, had a king paid out in this manner on behalf of his people.

Sugriva dared to criticise Corcoran for his generosity.

'I know exactly what I am doing,' said the Breton. 'Do you think I care about Holkar's millions, so harshly extorted from his own people? Sita, who is a better person than me, does not oppose my decision. Moreover, I suppose that, for lots of reasons, I will not reign for long and I am delighted to make the job of king so difficult that no one will dare or be able to do it after me.'

The sound of applause began to subside, and Corcoran was about to continue his speech, when a great uproar could be heard at the main entrance to the hall. The crowds of people parted, and they showed signs of great trepidation. Sugriva had moved towards the crowd to find out the cause of this disorder, while through the middle of the passage that had been created walked Louison, covered with blood and carrying between her teeth the inert body of Lakmana.

On seeing this, everyone began shouting with horror, and Corcoran himself seemed astonished.

Louison placed the Brahmin, who showed no signs of life, at the top of the steps leading to the throne. She then turned back where she had come from and signalled for her master to follow her. Already there were murmurings in the crowd, and talk of shooting the tigress to avenge the death of the Brahmin, but the Breton understood Louison's intentions and shouted that she was innocent and she was going to prove it.

And so she led Corcoran directly to Lakmana's house, took him down into the tunnel and showed him the barrels of gunpowder, the extinguished fuse and a dangerously wounded man, whose stomach had been opened up by the claws of Louison. This was the accomplice of the Brahmin, and he told Corcoran what had happened.

Louison had not died falling into the dungeons of the tower in Ayodhya. She had fallen in the way that all cats and tigers fall, on to her paws, but was dizzy, and almost fainted at the bottom of the terrifying chasm, which was covered with rocks and human bones. Once Lakmana had left, she regained her senses and did her best to reorient herself. Unfortunately, there were neither doors nor windows, unless one was sixty feet tall. That's the distance that separated her from the deadly trapdoor that had caused her downfall.

But Louison was not one to despair or leave her safety in the hands of the heavens or of chance. For three days and three nights she dug tirelessly in the earth and the rocks with her claws, having nothing to eat but half a dozen rats, which made her grimace, because she was refined, even a little spoilt. She only liked flowers and perfumes and the animals of the forest. However, she survived, that was the essential thing, and finally began to dig an underground tunnel as if she were a mole. After three days of relentless work, she once again saw sunlight, so dear to all living creatures, and found herself free about twenty paces from the ramparts of Ayodhya.

One can easily imagine the ardour with which she wished for vengeance. She ran straight to Bhagavpur and, without troubling herself with the celebrations, broke down the door of Lakmana's house with just one blow. She searched everywhere for the Brahmin, and discovered him in the tunnel, just at the moment when he was leaving after having set light to the fuse.

Seeing this, she leapt on Lakmana, knocking him over with one blow of her paw, and finished him off with her teeth, while wounding his accomplice – all within a few seconds. In the struggle, the fuse was extinguished (what good luck!), and Louison, very proud of her exploits, even if she wasn't aware of the full story, showed off what she had done to the assembly, as mentioned earlier, and thereby informed the people of Bhagavpur of the danger they had been in.

Is there any need to continue this story, to mention the great public joy, the coronation of Corcoran and Sita, and all the splendours that followed their coronation? One can imagine that Louison was not forgotten in the prayers which all the people offered up to Brahma and Vishnu, and it was believed, more than ever, that the Goddess Kali had taken the form of the tigress in order to appear among men.

The coronation festivities

Notes

1. This is a real institution, formed in 1700, which exists to this day under the name *Académie des Sciences, Belles-Lettres et Arts de Lyon.* In 1940, France's most senior Catholic priest, Cardinal Gerlier, on an official visit to the Academy in Lyon, embarrassed the Academicians by recalling these opening scenes of the novel. The disturbance caused by the dramatic appearance of Captain Corcoran and Louison at the Academy had, he said, 'haunted his childhood'.
2. There is no such text as the *Guru Karamta* (*Gouroukaramta* in French) – and the title appears to have been Assollant's invention. In several places later in the book he refers to the missing manuscript as *The Laws of Manu*, a genuine text better known now as the *Manusmriti* and which had, by Assollant's time, been translated into several European languages.

   The Ghats are the name of two ranges of mountains in India: the Eastern Ghats and the Western Ghats. Assollant is referring to the Western Ghats, which runs parallel to the coast of western India. The source of the Godavari River is in the Western Ghats, and in what used to be part of the Maratha Empire.
3. The Royal Asiatic Society was founded in Calcutta in 1784 by Sir William Jones, the translator of *The Laws of Manu* (see previous note).

4. Fans of the comic operas of Gilbert and Sullivan will recognise the name Captain Corcoran, who is the snobbish English captain in *HMS Pinafore*. It's not clear if this choice of name by W.S. Gilbert, who wrote the libretto for *HMS Pinafore* in 1877, was a pure coincidence, but it is worth noting that Gilbert spoke fluent French and travelled regularly to France in the years after the publication of Assollant's book.
5. The *Bhagavata Purana*: a real book written in Sanskrit, at some point between 500 and 1000 CE. It is probably the best known of the Puranas, and was translated into French prior to the publication of the first English translation – a matter of some pride to French orientalists, and perhaps the reason that Assollant chose this particular text for Corcoran to read.
6. The Presiding Officer was referring to the planet Neptune, whose position was predicted mathematically by the Frenchman Urbain Le Verrier in 1846, and identified later that year using a telescope by the German astrologer Johann Gottfried Galle.
7. All of these are real places, except for Baitpur which I have not been able to identify. In several of the places mentioned by Captain Corcoran, particularly those in southern India, Hindustani has never been widely spoken.
8. Robert Surcouf (1773–1827) was a well-known French privateer from Saint-Malo in Brittany, who captured ships from other countries with whom France was at a war. He became a hero in France during the Revolutionary and Napoleonic Wars, and French naval ships are still named after him. François, Viscount Chateaubriand (1768–1848), also born in Saint-Malo, was a royalist writer and politician who is usually considered the founder of the Romantic Movement in French literature. The other names mentioned in this paragraph are fictional, though Yves Quaterquem appears in other Assollant novels. Assollant is establishing Corcoran's republican heritage by referring to an invented altercation between Chateaubriand and Corcoran's great-uncle.

9. Saint-Nazaire is a coastal town in Brittany best known for shipbuilding. Batavia was the Dutch colonial name for what is now Jakarta, the capital of Indonesia.
10. Saint-Denis is now a northern suburb of Paris.
11. One of the 'grand boulevards' of central Paris, named after the Italian Theatre which was located there until the 1870s.
12. The Governor-General was the most senior British official in India, and was based in the capital of British India at that time, Calcutta. The names of the Governor-General, the Governor of Bombay and other British officials referred to in the book were invented by Assollant. The Governor General in 1857 was Viscount Canning.
13. Holkar is the family name of the Maharajahs of Indore, who ruled over one of India's most important princely states. Indore was part of the Maratha Confederacy which dominated much of central and western India between the late seventeenth and early nineteenth centuries. Following the defeat of Malhar Rao Holkar II by the British in the 3rd Maratha War of 1817–18, the Maharajahs of Indore accepted British suzerainty, and a British Resident was posted in the territory. Many Residents functioned as the unofficial rulers of the state in which they were posted. Bhagavpur is a fictional location which appears to be based on Maheshwar, the old fortified Holkar capital on the banks of the Narmada River.
14. Officially, in early 1857, it was not the British government which ruled large parts of India – but the East India Company, which had been set up as a British trading corporation under royal charter in 1600. After the Uprising of 1857, which is the context for the fictional events depicted in this book, the British Crown assumed responsibility for the East India Company's territories and armed forces in India.
15. Tippoo Sahib (1750–99), better known today as Tipu Sultan, was the ruler of the kingdom of Mysore, and an early ally of Napoleon. Tipu Sultan was defeated and killed by the British at

the Battle of Srirangapatnam (formerly Seringapatam) in 1799. His descendants were provided with pensions by the East India Company.

16. An anachronism. The post of Viceroy was only introduced in India after the events depicted in this book – that is, from November 1858.
17. At several points Assollant changes – perhaps deliberately, but more probably because he was writing in a hurry – the name of the book that Corcoran is searching for. Here, instead of *Guru Karamta* (or *Gouroukaramta* in French) he used the Sanskrit-sounding *Ramabagavattana* – which I have not been able to identify as a real book.
18. Tantia Tope (1814–59) was one of the leaders of the 1857 Uprising. He was executed by the British in 1859.
19. The first major act of rebellion of the 1857 Uprising took place in the northern city of Meerut in May, when what were known as 'native troops' mutinied, killed some British officers and their family members, and marched on Delhi.
20. Nana Sahib, the adopted son of the titular head of the Marathas. He became one of the best-known leaders of the 1857 Uprising, and disappeared soon after.
21. It's most unlikely that the son of a Parsi merchant would be called Rao, a Hindu name, used historically by, among others, the Holkar family. Holkar calls himself a Raghuvid, a descendant of Raghu, the grandfather of Dasharatha and the great-grandfather of Rama.
22. In the French text, at this point in the story, Assollant refers to the *Guru Karamta* as if it were the same text as *The Laws of Manu*, an early Sanskrit text which was by the mid-nineteenth century well known in Europe.
23. The speed of trains was, of course, not very fast in the mid-nineteenth century. A record of 82 miles per hour was set in Britain in the 1850s, and survived until the 1930s.
24. Sepoy was the name used to describe an Indian soldier in the

service of the British. In the nineteenth century, the 1857 Uprising was often referred to as the Sepoy Mutiny. The word sepoy or *sipahi* is still used to describe the lowest rank of soldier in the Indian army.

25. Assollant seems to have forgotten that a few pages earlier Robarts was arrested on the orders of Colonel Barclay and placed in detention for a month.
26. '*Goddam*' is a commonly used old French name for the English that goes back at least 500 years. It was said to have been coined in response to the 'Goddamn' curses of English soldiers on the battlefields of the Hundred Years' War.
27. Earlier, Sugriva describes himself as the messenger of Tantia Tope. Tope and Nana Sahib worked closely together.
28. Allsopp's India Pale Ale, brewed by Samuel Allsopp and Sons of Burton-on-Trent, was very popular in the subcontinent in the middle of the nineteenth century.
29. Clive was Lord Clive (1725–74), best known as 'Clive of India', who commanded the victorious British forces at the Battle of Plassey (1757), and returned to Britain as an extremely rich man. Hastings was Warren Hastings (1732–1818) who was effectively the first British Governor-General of India (though the specific title did not then exist). He also made a fortune during his time in India, and was tried (impeached) and acquitted of a wide variety of crimes and misdemeanours on his return to Britain. The word 'nabob' was a British mishearing of the imperial Mughal title 'Nawab'. In the nineteenth-century Europe, nabobs were rich Europeans who had made their fortunes in India.
30. Assollant mistakenly refers to the good Baronet as Sir Richard Barrowlinson at this point in the text.
31. Arthur Wellesley, Duke of Wellington (1769–1852), the younger brother of a Governor-General of India, first made his name as military officer in the campaign against Tipu Sultan in 1799, and in the 2nd Maratha War of 1803–05. Wellesley returned to Europe and, and as the Duke of Wellington, led the British

forces to victory over Napoleon at Waterloo. Wellington was also twice British prime minister.

32. Assollant appears to have forgotten that earlier he described the staircase in the temple as leading downwards, not up.
33. The name that Corcoran used here for the elephant, 'Scindia', is in fact the family name of the Maharajahs of Gwalior, who ruled another large Maratha principality.
34. Timur – better known in the west as Tamburlaine (died 1405) or, in French, Tamerlan – was the founder of the Timurid Empire which controlled much of Central Asia and Persia in the fourteenth and fifteenth centuries. Timur invaded India and captured Delhi in 1398. The Maratha Confederacy did not exist at the time of Timur's invasion.
35. An overland crossing of Egypt was necessary because the Suez Canal only opened in 1869 – twelve years after the events that Assollant is describing, and two years after the publication of *The Adventures of Captain Corcoran.*
36. The mutiny in Meerut began on 9 May 1857. Some of the rebels reached Delhi the following day and would soon proclaim the ailing Mughal Emperor Bahadur Shah Zafar as their leader. It took until September for the British to defeat the rebels. The last Mughal emperor was exiled to Burma, and three of his sons were executed.
37. The Seine heads south-west from the Pont de la Concorde in central Paris before making an enormous loop back north-east to reach the northern suburb of Saint-Denis. The journey between the two places referred to by Assollant is eight kilometres by road, but more than twenty-five kilometres by river.
38. The Anglo-Sikh wars were fought in the 1840s, and led to the dismemberment of the Sikh empire in Punjab and the rest of north-west India. Captain Bangor is an invented character.
39. Lord Palmerston was the British Prime Minister at the time of the 1857 Uprising.
40. The French language saying 'Dieu et mon Droit', which literally

means 'God and my right', is the motto of the British monarch. It was first used by Richard I of England, whose main language was French, in the twelfth century.

41. Empyrean Heaven: the highest part of heaven, where the gods dwell.
42. Unlike all the other names of British soldiers mentioned by Assollant, Sir Henry Lawrence did exist. The British had annexed the kingdom of Oudh (or Avadh) in 1856, and exiled its king. Its capital, Lucknow, became the scene of the most drawn-out of all the confrontations of the 1857 Uprising. The siege of Lucknow lasted almost six months, and the British commander Sir Henry Lawrence died in the siege.
43. Assollant inserted the not entirely accurate parenthetical description of *zamindars* as district governors into the text. *Zamindars* were usually landowning aristocrats with hereditary title to their estates. Princely rulers used *zamindars* as a means of exerting authority and collecting taxes.
44. Assollant has forgotten that Sugriva has only recently met Holkar, more recently than Corcoran.
45. Assollant has a footnote to the original text stating that 80 million rupees are worth 320 million francs.
46. Aurangzeb (1618–1707) was in fact the third of four sons of the Mughal Emperor Shah Jahan and his wife Mumtaz Mahal. He did lock up his father – in the fort at Agra. Aurangzeb also had two of his brothers murdered, and the third was killed in what is now Burma on the orders of a local prince while he was fleeing Aurangzeb's army.
47. The Jagannath temple in the city of Puri in eastern India – where entry is forbidden to non-Hindus.
48. Now better known as the Malaysian peninsula.

A Note on the Translator

Sam Miller was born and brought up in London, but has spent much of his adult life in India. He is a former BBC journalist, and author of *Delhi: Adventures in a Megacity* and *A Strange Kind of Paradise: India Through Foreign Eyes*.

CRAFTED FOR MOBILE READING

Thought you would never read a book on mobile? Let us prove you wrong.

AN EXTENSIVE LIBRARY

Including fresh, new, original Juggernaut books from the likes of Sunny Leone, Praveen Swami, Husain Haqqani, Umera Ahmed, Rujuta Diwekar and lots more. Plus, books from partner publishers and loads of free classics. Whichever genre you like, there's a book waiting for you.

juggernaut.in

DON'T JUST READ; INTERACT

We're changing the reading experience from passive to active.

Ask authors questions

Get all your answers from the horse's mouth. Juggernaut authors actually reply to every question they can.

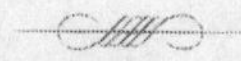

Rate and review

Let everyone know of your favourite reads or critique the finer points of a book – you will be heard in a community of like-minded readers.

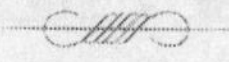

Gift books to friends

For a book-lover, there's no nicer gift than a book personally picked. You can even do it anonymously if you like.

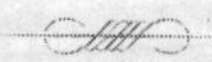

Enjoy new book formats

Discover serials released in parts over time, picture books including comics, and story-bundles at discounted rates. And coming soon, audiobooks.

LOWEST PRICES & ONE-TAP BUYING

Books start at ₹10 with regular discounts and free previews.

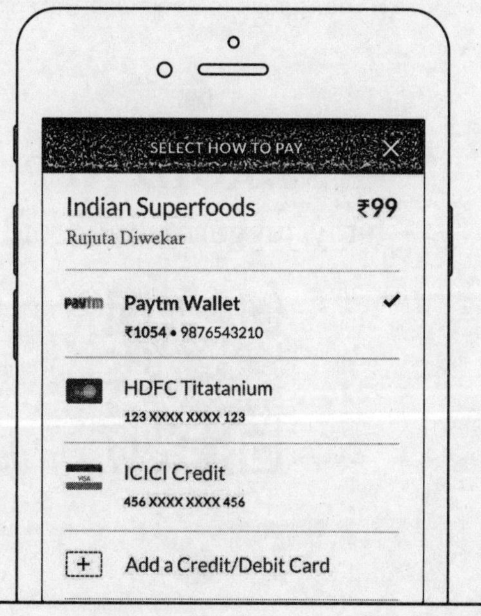

Paytm Wallet, Cards & Apple Payments

On Android, just add a Paytm Wallet once and buy any book with one tap. On iOS, pay with one tap with your iTunes-linked debit/credit card.

Click the QR Code with a QR scanner app or type the link into the Internet browser on your phone to download the app.

ANDROID APP

bit.ly/juggernautandroid

iOS APP

bit.ly/juggernautios

For our complete catalogue, visit www.juggernaut.in
To submit your book, send a synopsis and two sample chapters to books@juggernaut.in
For all other queries, write to contact@juggernaut.in